DISCARD

Look Back on Death

As Dell Shannon:

CASE PENDING
THE ACE OF SPADES
EXTRA KILL
KNAVE OF HEARTS
DEATH OF A BUSYBODY
DOUBLE BLUFF
ROOT OF ALL EVIL
MARK OF MURDER
THE DEATH-BRINGERS
DEATH BY INCHES
COFFIN CORNER
WITH A VENGEANCE
CHANCE TO KILL

RAIN WITH VIOLENCE
KILL WITH KINDNESS
SCHOOLED TO KILL
CRIME ON THEIR HANDS
UNEXPECTED DEATH
WHIM TO KILL
THE RINGER
MURDER WITH LOVE
WITH INTENT TO KILL
NO HOLIDAY FOR CRIME
SPRING OF VIOLENCE
CRIME FILE
DEUCES WILD

As Elizabeth Linington:

PERCHANCE OF DEATH
THE PROUD MAN
THE LONG WATCH
MONSIEUR JANVIER
THE KINGBREAKER
POLICEMAN'S LOT
ELIZABETH I (*Encyc. Brit.*)

GREENMASK!
NO EVIL ANGEL
DATE WITH DEATH
SOMETHING WRONG
PRACTISE TO DECEIVE
CRIME BY CHANCE

As Egan O'Neill:

THE ANGLOPHILE

As Lesley Egan:

A CASE FOR APPEAL
THE BORROWED ALIBI
AGAINST THE EVIDENCE
RUN TO EVIL
MY NAME IS DEATH
DETECTIVE'S DUE
A SERIOUS INVESTIGATION
THE WINE OF VIOLENCE

IN THE DEATH OF A MAN
MALICIOUS MISCHIEF
PAPER CHASE
SCENES OF CRIME
THE BLIND SEARCH
A DREAM APART
LOOK BACK ON DEATH

Look Back on Death

LESLEY EGAN

PUBLISHED FOR THE CRIME CLUB BY
DOUBLEDAY & COMPANY, INC.
GARDEN CITY, NEW YORK
1978

ISBN: 0-385-14303-6
Library of Congress Catalog Card Number 77–27725
Copyright © 1978 by Elizabeth Linington
All Rights Reserved
Printed in the United States of America
First Edition

For Margaret Van Tine—
a most loyal friend and fan

But how is it
That this lives in thy mind? What seest thou else
In the dark backward and abysm of time?
—*The Tempest*   act 1, scene 2

ONE

Sergeant Andrew Clock, Hollywood division, L.A.P.D., together with his wife Fran, had been visiting his brother- and sister-in-law, Jesse and Nell Falkenstein. On the point of departure, he looked at Jesse with something less than love and said, "Well, I'll read your damned books some time when I get round to it. Do I thank you?"

"Probably," said Jesse acidly.

Fran and Nell exchanged a glance. "You shouldn't have gone tramping all over my big brother's convictions," said Fran lightly. "Come on, Andrew, it's beginning to rain."

Clock growled and turned from the open front door; in the little drizzle they hurried to the car in the driveway. Jesse shut the front door and Nell said, "You needn't have jumped all over him like that. After all, it's a—a specialized subject. Why should a cop know anything about parapsychology? Cops deal in plain facts."

"That's right!" said Jesse violently. "Get me all set to deliver another lecture to you! Damn it, that's just the point—facts. What else, for God's sake, is the entire field of research dealing in? For nearly a hundred years a long list of respected scientists have been meticulously turning up the plain facts—the documented solid facts of telepathy, clairvoyance, mediumship, precognition, psychokinesis, and all the rest of it, and publishing the reams of solid evidence. And yet the ordinary average intelligent man like Andrew doesn't know one damned thing about it. It's stupid."

"Riding your hobby horse," said Nell. "Why should he? We're living in the nuclear age, and I like to think I'm reasonably intelligent but I don't know anything about atoms or fission."

"Survival of the individual soul is slightly more important," said Jesse, but reluctantly he grinned. "I'll educate the man yet. Him and his don't confuse me with facts, my mind's made up." He started to switch off lamps in the living room. Nell laughed and took Athelstane the mastiff to the back door, let him out for a last run. She looked in on the baby down the hall; at nearly ten months of age, David Andrew had mercifully learned to sleep at night. As she came into the bedroom Jesse was shedding watch and loose change on the bureau top. "You want me to look at this place in Studio City?"

"Not really. I don't like it that well." Nell sounded dissatisfied. "I suppose I'll find something sometime. Only the prices are ridiculous. I wonder if we ought to get a bigger place, Jesse."

"I don't," said Jesse, "need a direct-voice communication from the old man to tell me he meant us to use the money and have fun with it. Don't fuss, Nell. Only money—what he'd tell you—and it can go as easy as it comes, so we might as well enjoy it." He yawned, reaching for his pajamas.

Old Mr. Walters had died last May and left Jesse a respectable amount of money. The will had finally got through probate last month. The first fun they'd had with it was the new cars, which they'd both badly needed—two brand-new Mercedes. And as Nell said, this house was in a fairly good older section of Hollywood, but if they were going to have at least one more and possibly two in the family, it would be nice to have a bigger house with more space around it for Athelstane. She'd started looking at houses last week, but so far hadn't found any she liked.

When she emerged from the bathroom to find Jesse sitting up in bed smoking over a copy of *Hidden Channels of the Mind*, she sat down at the dressing table and said thoughtfully, "He would be pleased, wouldn't he? It is what he'd have wanted us to do." She let her hair down, the dark-brown mass of hair never cut, and began to brush it quickly.

"No would be about it, he's probably keeping an eye on us and getting a kick out of it. Maybe he'll pick out a house and lead you to it some way."

Nell laughed, starting to braid her hair. "I wouldn't put it past him."

"Somebody's said, money isn't everything but it can make you damned comfortable. But we needn't let it go to our heads. Office hours as usual—it could all go down the drain tomorrow, and I've got some new clients coming in. I suppose you'll be out with your realtors."

"Not if it's pouring like this. Do you realize it's past midnight? You and Andrew going at it hammer and tongs like that —I'll get Athelstane in."

"Mmh." Jesse put down his book and reached for the lamp switch. "And I've got to be in court at ten." He was never operating on all cylinders before noon.

But when he got to his office, in the new tall building on Wilshire, he was informed by his twin secretaries, Jean and Jimmy Gordon, that Mrs. Thomas had called in at eight-thirty, and there'd be no court session; there'd been a reconciliation. "They're all lovey-dovey again and she wants you to kill the divorce petition."

"These females," said Jesse.

"There's not much else for you this morning—paperwork on the probate for the Gorham will, and you said to remind you about getting the court order to sell the stock, to get the inheritance tax cleared out of the way. You've got an appointment at ten, this Mr. and Mrs. Tredgold."

"Did they say what about?"

"Not a word."

"O.K., shoot them in when they get here." Jesse looked approvingly at the Gordons, identical brown-eyed blondes and very efficient girls, and went on into his office. The new office was a good deal handsomer than the old one, with its smooth paneling, the austere Holbein portrait of Sir Thomas More on one wall, lush carpeting, the big desk; and all the gadgets, like the tape recorder and the calculator, were useful. He pulled out the recorder and dictated a letter about the court order, which brought him to nine-fifteen. He hadn't started to draw up that Wallingford will; he got out the notes he'd taken yesterday and glanced through them, sliding a new tape into the recorder. After raining all night, it had let up this morning; now it was starting again, a slithery shushing against the windows.

He thought, a slow day, not much to do; he might drop in to see if DeWitt had anything interesting on hand this afternoon. William DeWitt, happily pottering around with his Western Association for Psychic Research, could always be relied on for some interesting talk at any rate.

The new clients were more than prompt; Jimmy looked in at a quarter of ten to tell him the Tredgolds were here. Jesse told her to send them in.

The first impression he got from them was Money. They were a good-looking couple, quietly well dressed, smart, smooth, discreet, nothing flashy. The man was tall, with good shoulders, nearly crew-cut dark hair, firm mouth, rather cynical dark eyes; his gray suit hadn't come off a rack, and his tie was a Sulka. He might be forty. She was a little younger, dark hair, with a nice figure, very fair complexion, and intensely blue eyes; her clothes so quietly smart that they were unobtrusive. And both of them looked troubled and worried, as people who came to see a lawyer sometimes did.

Jesse had stood up; Tredgold offered him a firm hand. "Sit down, won't you? What can I do for you?"

They sat down in two of the leather-upholstered chairs and Tredgold said, "I don't know." He had a deep voice; he looked and sounded like a man usually very sure of himself but now annoyed because for some reason he wasn't. "I don't know if you can do anything at all, but we thought we'd come and ask."

"Because the company lawyers wouldn't be any use," said Mrs. Tredgold. "And of course Mr. Featherstone's dead. Not

that I ever thought he was much use either. You know I said at
the time, Walt, we should have got someone younger—more,
oh, up and coming." She looked at Jesse. "You see, we happen
to know Ray Austin, Mr. Falkenstein."

It took Jesse ten seconds to identify the name, and then he
said, "Oh, really." His mind slid back to that little affair: one of
the cases where old Edgar Walters' knowledge of human nature
had spotted the place to look for truth. "How is he these
days?"

"Far as I know, fine." Tredgold was impatient. "He never
can say enough about you. We just thought, ask what you
think." He got out cigarettes, gave one to his wife, lit both. He
looked at his cigarette, evidently unsure momentarily how to
proceed, and then he asked baldly, "Is there any legal way to
force a man to go on parole?"

Jesse stared at him curiously. "Generally speaking, anybody
qualified for parole's happy to get it."

"I know, I know, but it's a hell of a situation, and we just
don't know what to do about it. *Is* there any way?"

"Maybe you'd better tell me something about the circumstances, Mr. Tredgold," said Jesse gently.

"Yes, of course, I suppose you'll have to know the whole
story," said Tredgold unhappily. "It's my brother Dick. He's
put in seven and a half years, he's up for parole, and the
damned fool won't take it. We've both argued with him—damn
it, I can see how he feels in a way, but it's water under the
bridge, and a smart man knows when to cut his losses. He's
only thirty-five, he's got the other half of his life to live, and
God knows there's enough money waiting—I've looked after it
like my own. You can't spend that kind of money in jail, and
I've got a smart stockbroker. This damn fool brother of mine's
got half a million bucks waiting for him, and his old job back—
even after all the money I spent on lawyers trying to get what
she left him in her will. Thank God," said Tredgold devoutly,
"all the company stock was tied up in trust under Uncle Walt's
will. If she'd owned that outright and split it between us, and
the state claimed he couldn't profit by the death—my God.

What a mess that would have been. As it was—" He seemed to think he was explaining.

"Excuse me," said Jesse. "Money from where?"

"Oh. Chain of markets," said Tredgold. "The Super-T's. Our uncle—Walter Tredgold—started out with one little place thirty-five, forty years back. He was a good businessman and he was lucky. We've got twenty-one supermarts now, all over the place from Thousand Oaks to Santa Monica. Dick and I got 40 per cent of the company stock when he died fourteen years ago. He was smart enough to tie up the rest in trust, what he left Aunt Lou. She"—he smiled a little—"didn't have much head for money. On her death the rest of the stock was split between Dick and me, but that wasn't anything to do with her will, you see, so that was all right. She had the entire income but she couldn't touch the principal."

"Where does the parole come in?" asked Jesse. "What's your brother in for?"

Tredgold leaned back. "Homicide. You don't remember the case? It was eight and a half years ago—"

"Afraid not."

"There was an appeal—it all took so damned much time— but it was turned down. And then all the legal fuss—"

"It was a nightmare," said Mrs. Tredgold in her light, pretty voice. She put out her cigarette; her hand was shaking. "Just thinking about it brings it all back. All the little things. Do you know, I've never been able to read a detective novel since. Murder—it's not a thing you expect to happen, and maybe in a book motives and alibis and witnesses are interesting, but when it's real— There was all that blood on the carpet, and you couldn't just leave it, even when we knew the house would be sold. And sorting out all her things, I couldn't expect Alida to help—and Dick in jail, and then she lost the baby, we'd all been so happy about the baby—"

"Oh, Becky, don't go *over* it!" said Tredgold roughly. "It was the worst time any of us lived through, but it's over. It's happened. What we have to think about now is Dick."

"Your brother was charged with murdering this aunt?" asked Jesse. "First degree?"

"No. It wasn't—nobody ever thought it was premeditated. It was second degree, he got twenty to thirty years. I—"

Jesse's eyebrows shot up. "Stiff sentence for second degree homicide."

Tredgold's mouth hardened. After a moment he said, "That judge— There was a lot of subtle harping on the money, the other side tried to make it look as if we were—oh, café society, bunch of snobs who'd never done a day's good work. My God, you've got to run a business—what do they think the manager of a big company does all day? Dick and I both worked an eight-hour day, Uncle Walt sent both of us right through the business, since we turned fifteen and started out as bag boys. I ought to tell you that our parents were killed in an air crash when I was twelve and Dick was eight, and Uncle Walt and Aunt Lou brought us up—they never had any children. Dad was a GP, but he'd only been in practice for five years, and with working his way through medical school, he didn't leave much. How the hell did I get on this? Oh, the money. Hell, Dick and I held every job there is, getting experience to run the business —bag boy, checkout clerk, stock clerk, on up. We've both got degrees in business management. I'm sorry, all this is irrelevant, didn't I just say it's water under the bridge? Just, we always felt the judge was—prejudiced. He was dead against Dick in his instructions to the jury, and—well, that was how it came out, twenty to thirty, and the appeal turned down."

"A nightmare," repeated his wife, her eyes still shut. "And it didn't end. It was just before Christmas, you know. That the trial ended. With all that—the sentence, and Alida losing the baby—we had to do something about Christmas, because Judy and Jim were just little things, six and four, you couldn't disappoint them. Dick and Alida had just bought a house—they'd only been married a year—and after the miscarriage and then the appeal getting denied she couldn't bear to live there, and we found her an apartment. It was all the little things, things you don't think about—getting special permission to see Dick because we needed his signature on the escrow papers— And we thought he was going to be sent to the prison at Susanville, and oh, God, if he only had been. If he only had—"

"Shut up, Becky," said Tredgold, but he said it kindly. "I've said it before, free will I believe in up to a point. There is such a thing as fate. If he'd been in Susanville, Alida wouldn't have made that drive once a month, I'll grant you. She'd have flown instead, and you're likelier to get killed in an airplane than in a car."

"She was killed." Jesse was patiently following the thread of story.

"The year afterward," said Tredgold. "On her way up the coast to visit him. Drunk rammed her car head-on."

"He could have a visitor once a month," said his wife. "And the letters, of course. But after that—"

"It was easier," said Tredgold unexpectedly. "I won't say it wasn't easier. Alida'd been there all the while, keeping us reminded. You can see we'd felt a responsibility, we'd check on her, have her over, do things for her. She hadn't any family here—her mother was dead, her father lived in Maine. And after she was gone, it got a little easier. Dick—just wasn't there. Oh, we kept in touch—regular letters, I kept him up on the business. I got his power of attorney to deal with his share of the stock and so on. For quite a while even after Alida was killed he kept up his interest—followed the stock market, he'd ask me to buy into this or sell that for him. But lately, no. I don't know what's got into the damned fool. He knew he could get parole after seven years."

"It's on account of Alida," said his wife. "Mostly, I think. He feels he hasn't got anything waiting."

"He's got the hell of a lot waiting," said Tredgold angrily. "He's still a young man. He's got us, his whole family. Enough money. He knows how much we think of him, for God's sake. It's just his damned stubbornness—Dick always was pig-headed, get an idea into his head and you can't move him—"

"But just exactly why doesn't he want to accept parole, Mr. Tredgold?" asked Jesse. "You've lost me. Seems to me, way you put it, it's water under the bridge all right. And just what do you want me to do about it?"

"He says"—Tredgold, who had been leaning forward, flung himself back in his chair looking disgusted—"it's the principle of the thing. He says if he accepts parole, it would be a tacit admission that he was guilty, that everything he testified to at the trial was a lie, and he won't do it. He says it's just too damn bad for the judge and jury who said he was guilty, but that's not his fault—but if he takes parole, he'd be partly to blame too. Principle!" Tredgold uttered the word as if it were an oath. "Throwing away the rest of his life for a silly damned idea like that—"

"Well, legally speaking, when the court found him guilty . . ." began Jesse, and Becky Tredgold interrupted him in a surprised tone.

"Oh, we all knew he wasn't guilty, Mr. Falkenstein. You don't suppose we ever thought— Of course Dick couldn't possibly have killed Aunt Lou." She read his careful expression uncannily and added, "You're thinking an innocent man couldn't have been convicted?"

"It happens," said Jesse. "Not very often. More likely, in our judicial system, the other way round, Mrs. Tredgold. But I don't say it can't happen."

"The trouble was," said Tredgold, "it didn't look as if anybody else could have done it. Only we knew he didn't. But that's over, and when he's got a new life ahead— I don't know what the hell I expect you to do about it."

"But Ray Austin," said Becky Tredgold, "seems to think you're some kind of miracle worker, Mr. Falkenstein. He told us all about how you got him out of trouble, when his wife was murdered. What I thought was—you're an outsider. A stranger to Dick. If you just went to see him, and talked quiet common sense to him—you don't have any ax to grind, it's nothing to do with you at all. And I know how it's gone with those two—"

She looked at her husband with a faint smile. "Walt starting out trying to be calm and sensible, and the more Dick digs his heels in the madder Walt gets, so he ends up yelling at him and Dick getting all the more stubborn."

"Well—" Jesse shrugged. "I don't know what I could accomplish, but if you're willing to invest in a retainer and expenses I can go talk to him. As his accredited lawyer, I suppose I'll be let in. Where is he?"

"In the Men's Colony at San Luis Obispo. How much do you want?" Tredgold already had a checkbook out.

"Oh, nominal retainer—a hundred bucks. That's only about a four-hour drive up the coast."

"Obviously, I can't advise you on what to say. But if you can make him see what a damn fool he is—" Tredgold stood up and laid the check on Jesse's desk.

"Just hope you're not expecting too much." Jesse went to open the office door for them. "I had some luck—and some help —on Mr. Austin's affair, you know."

Mrs. Tredgold smiled at him suddenly. "You're not at all the way I pictured you. From what Ray said, I thought you'd be a live wire, tearing around terrifically full of energy. But I had a feeling about it. About coming to you. I'm not at all psychic, but now and then I get a feeling, that's all." She turned her back to her husband and he helped her into her smart blue raincoat, picked up his own.

"See what happens," said Jesse. "I'll be in touch with you."

They nodded at him and went out. "At least," said Jimmy after them, "new clients with money, by their clothes."

"Jamesina," said Jesse absently, "you are a mercenary Scot. Funny new clients, if you want to know. What time is it?" It was eleven-thirty. "What have I got on the agenda in the next couple of days?"

Jean flipped her desk pad. "Mrs. Barnes is coming in at three o'clock." And Jesse didn't look forward to seeing her, poor woman: she was unhappy about getting her senile mother declared incompetent, but she hadn't any choice. "Nothing else today, no appointments tomorrow—you thought the Thomas divorce was going to be contested, and left the day open. Nothing on Thursday until the afternoon, Mr. Page."

"Mmh," said Jesse. "Except all the paperwork which you two can do. I'm going out for an early lunch. We'll get the Wallingford will drawn this afternoon. Meanwhile you can get hold of the warden's office at the California Men's Colony at San Luis Obispo and intimate that I want a chat with him at whatever convenient time today. About legal visitation rights to Mr. Richard Tredgold."

It wasn't often that either of the Gordons, cool and experienced legal secretaries, showed astonishment; they did now. "A relative of *theirs?*" asked Jimmy, glancing at the door the Tredgolds had just exited. "In prison? For heaven's sake—they look so utterly respectable."

"Which they seem to be," agreed Jesse.

He dropped into the coffee shop down the block for a ham sandwich and coffee, and drove up to Santa Monica Boulevard to the modest headquarters of DeWitt's association. After years of psychic research carried out on other researchers' ideas, DeWitt was now his own man, and a happy one. He had enough money of his own; a couple of wealthy friends supported the project, paid the rent and modest fees to his psychics, and the terrifyingly efficient Miss Duffy was accumulating stacks of precise records in a battery of file cases. He had four psychics at his beck and call: Mrs. Ventnor producing the automatic writing, Wanda Moreno and Cora Delaney as trance mediums, and the psychometrist Charles MacDonald.

Jesse sniffed at the latest pages of automatic script. "Nothing significant to you?" asked DeWitt rather wistfully. He was aware that Jesse would welcome some communication. He looked at Jesse enquiringly, a man as tall and dark and lanky as Jesse, and his long nose twitched over the scrawled page.

"Don't much like the automatic writing anyway," said Jesse. "Suspect production of the subconscious."

"Some wheat in the chaff," said DeWitt. "We had a very good session with Cora last night—some very evidential material. I've got it all on tape, have you time to listen to it?"

"Probably not," said Jesse. "Let me take it home."

"You're the only man I'd let take records out of the office. For twenty-four hours."

"Cross my heart, you'll get it back safe." Jesse put the tape in his breast pocket. "I'd better get back to work."

Back in his own office, he found that Jean had arranged for him to talk to the warden at three o'clock. He spent an hour dictating Mr. Wallingford's will, Jimmy typed it, and he proofread it. At three o'clock precisely Jean looked in and said she had the warden's office on hold. They were really marvelous girls, his Gordons, reflected Jesse, picking up the phone. Ever since they'd come to him he had felt cherished; they could probably run the office without him.

He got home early at five o'clock, and found Athelstane huddled lonesomely on the back porch, his black-jowled face anxious. It was still raining steadily. "I thought she said she wasn't going in the rain," said Jesse to Athelstane. Athelstane followed him in happily and sat on his feet while Jesse built himself a drink. But Nell drove in five minutes later and fled in the back door with a howling baby in her arms.

"It wasn't supposed to rain, according to the radio," she said crossly, handing David Andrew to Jesse while she took off her coat. "It hadn't started when I left, and the realtor at Red Carpet had these places I wanted to see, so I left the baby with Fran and just went, and one thing led to another and I saw six impossible houses— Here, I'd better feed him first."

"Well, you won't have to worry about getting dinner for me tomorrow night, you can gad around as you please. I'm leaving you temporarily."

"Who for?" asked Nell interestedly.

"Wrong pronoun. What. I've got to drive up to San Luis to see an inmate of the prison colony. Funny business." He told her about it after she'd shut off the baby's bellows with a pacifying bottle.

"I don't know what they think a lawyer can do, if the man's made up his mind," said Nell. "Funny isn't the word. Oh, Fran said to tell you that Andrew hasn't looked at your books yet but she was finding the Archer book very interesting."*

"That's nice," said Jesse. Fran, of course, didn't need convincing about the reality of psychic phenomena. "Glad I provided her with entertainment while she tended the little monster."

"He was good as gold," said Nell reproachfully, "but I was later than I intended and naturally he was starved. And so am I, and probably you—I'll use the microwave. The money is useful, isn't it?"

It was. Very nice indeed. And Jesse could almost see the old man, chuckling and pleased to see them enjoying it. The Mercedes, elegantly modeled, sleek and silver-gray, was a very nice girl to drive. On a weekday there wasn't much traffic on the coast highway, once you got out of the suburban sprawl that was Los Angeles and environs. He might have made it up and back in one day, but if it was still raining he'd as soon not drive south at night; there would be fog along this road, which followed the Pacific coast most of the way.

Even in the thin drizzle he rather enjoyed the drive, getting out of the city to the bare lonely rounded hills with red-and-white cattle grazing and always on his left a gray cold sea with the white line of breakers. After he by-passed Santa Barbara the country was even emptier, the towns smaller. Living in the teeming dirty sprawl of Los Angeles, you forgot that California was the foremost agricultural state in the nation; here, these broad fields and hills, the cattle, the lush greenery of upstanding crops, were a reminder.

He had never laid eyes on this state prison; "at San Luis" might mean anything. He stopped at the courthouse to ask directions: the Men's Colony was further up the coast toward

* *Crime and the Psychic World.*

Morro Bay. It was two forty-five when he came on it. It was a rather drab-looking but surprisingly casual set of buildings, no walls around it: this was medium security. There was a succession of white-painted cottages attached, a big central building block. A security guard at the gate took his name, used a phone, let him in; this wasn't a regular day for visitors. "That's right, sir," he said, putting down the phone. "You can park over here." Jesse was turned over to another uniformed guard, who took him into the central building. Down a long bare corridor he was led into a curious place where small cubicles were boarded off by plywood panels. The guard shut the door behind him. The cubicle was perhaps four feet square; there was a straight chair in it, a glass ashtray on a narrow counter facing him, and nothing else. Across the counter was set a metal grill rising to the low ceiling, and on its other side was another straight chair, a cubicle, a door.

Jesse sat down and lit a cigarette. Five minutes later, the door opened on the other side of the grille and a man came into the other cubicle. He stood there with his back against the door and surveyed Jesse with indifferent curiosity.

"Not the regular day for visitors," he said. "Old Paddy said my lawyer'd come to see me. News to me I had a lawyer—I thought old Featherstone was dead. Who might you be?"

Jesse slid a card under the one narrow opening in the grille. Richard Tredgold, oddly, looked younger than thirty-five. There was a general resemblance to his brother: he was tall and dark, with dark eyes under sharp-arched brows, but his face was leaner, paler, with a cleft chin. His eyes were brilliantly alive. He was wearing a drab-olive cotton shirt and slacks. He picked up the card and smiled at it.

"Let me guess. They've sent you up to reason with me, since Walt can't keep his temper long enough to do it himself. They must think you're a persuasive orator, Mr. Falkenstein."

"I didn't think it was such a good idea myself," said Jesse mildly. "Wouldn't say oratory's my strongest point. They picked me because they happen to know a fellow I once rescued from a murder charge. Judgment slightly biased, shall we say."

"Oh?" Tredgold looked more interested. "A murder charge. You must be reasonably persuasive at that."

"Oh, it didn't come to a trial. The police were a bit hasty—evidence, but when I poked around some I found some other evidence and we came up with the real X."

Tredgold sat down on the straight chair and reached to his breast pocket for a pack of cigarettes, a book of matches. "This is a fairly decent place," he said. "We're allowed reasonable amenities. Ten cigarettes a day, if you can afford them. Walt sends more money than I can use, so I'm quite popular with a lot of poor devils who never have visitors or presents. Do you know something funny, Mr. Falkenstein? I've learned a lot here. Before, I never read much. Boned up the textbooks in college, that was all—I never had time. Here, I've discovered books. I've spent seven years reading everything I could lay my hands on. They've been pretty nice to me, gone out of the way to get me books I wanted. The last year or so I've been studying metaphysics, and I suppose you could say it's induced a philosophical calm over me. Time is but the stream I go a-fishing in, as it were. This can be a very contemplative life, if you take it that way. The last couple of years I've been in charge of the library. I enjoy that."

"Yes, but when Thoreau said that about time, he was alone and free, living a contemplative life he'd chosen," said Jesse softly.

Tredgold's face was mobile; his eyes flickered, his mouth twisted, and he said, "*Touché.* But you might understand my lunatic principles, which dear good old Walt never in this world will. A judge and jury said I was guilty of murder, which I wasn't. If I accepted parole now—I have really confounded poor Warden Miles, he's had me up for a number of bluff man-to-man talks, and he keeps saying, but you're an intelligent man—if I took parole, I would be in effect saying, they were quite right, I was guilty, and having served a token sentence I acknowledge it. I won't do that."

"Biting off your nose to spite your face?" said Jesse to his cigarette.

Dick Tredgold laughed. "I know what Walt and Becky said

to you. They're such dear good people. I won't tell you that if Alida were still waiting, I wouldn't—cut my losses, as Walt puts it. But she's not. Looking back, it was like Nemesis— everything going wrong at once. Maybe a karmic debt from some past life? I wouldn't know. Do you know anything about the murder at all? About the evidence?"

"Not a thing."

"So you're thinking, there must have been some good evidence, or I wouldn't be here. There was. On the evidence, it didn't look as if anybody else could have done it. I know I didn't, but I'm the only one who does know that. People do kill their nearest and dearest—some people. They made a lot of that at the trial, that Aunt Lou had been like my own mother— I was eight when Walt and I went to live with them. Yes. She was." He laughed suddenly, and his tone was queerly tender. "Of course we were both furious with her—we'd both had some hot and heavy arguments with her. Silly darling little old Aunt Lou, taking up another fad—under the spell of this damned so-called psychic and proposing to hand the woman fifty G's, I ask you. I had another argument with her that day, surely to God. And all that testimony about my hot temper—" He leaned back in the chair, smiling. "But oddly enough, everything old Featherstone said about my not being able to kill Aunt Lou was gospel truth."

"Only the jury didn't believe it," said Jesse.

"Or the judge. I can't say I care whether you believe it," said Tredgold coolly. "It really doesn't matter. Aunt Lou knows I didn't do it, and I know." Suddenly he gave Jesse a wide grin. "I'll tell you something, Mr. Falkenstein. That fellow you mentioned—who sent Walt and Becky to you—you playing private eye to find the real killer. Well, you go and find out who really murdered Aunt Lou, and prove it—prove that I didn't do it, so the governor'll put it on paper that I didn't do it. That's the only way I'm going to leave this place. Only, of course, I don't suppose you ever could. Walt had a private detective agency on it, and they never turned up anything."

"Didn't you have any ideas?" asked Jesse.

"Negative. Aunt Lou? Beaten to death with the poker in her own living room? It wasn't a thing that could happen. We have movies every Saturday night," said Tredgold, sounding a little tired. "Sometimes old movies. And Aunt Lou—she was Billie Burke. You know? The fantastic hats, and the shopping expeditions with the girl friends, much the same kind, and she may have been a little silly and frivolous and zany, but she had the kindest heart in the world. We were mad as hell at her, and she was mad at us—but it was family," said Tredgold simply. He looked at Jesse with a return to cool indifference and laughed soundlessly.

"Walt sending you—it has its funny side. Well, that's my word on it. If you want to play detective and try to find out the truth—get some solid evidence— But after eight years, the thing's absurd. Water under the bridge—I'll bet Walt said that, all right. It's impossible, we'll never know what happened." Tredgold stood up abruptly. "You'd better go back to Walt and tell him to forget it."

"I am fairly conscientious," said Jesse. "I like at least to earn my retainers."

TWO

"Just the one word he said, you know. Family. Anybody from any sized family—maybe not you—would understand that." Nell had been a very lonely only child. "The fights Fran and I had—the hot fights in any family—but nothing to lead to homicide. Only that could be difficult to get across to cops when a real homicide happened."

"Now really," said Nell. "You're not going to get mixed up in this ancient history, Jesse? Just on impulse?"

"Impulse be damned. I'm just a little curious," said Jesse. "I'd like to have a look at the trial transcript before I see the Tredgolds again."

"Honestly, the things you get into," said Nell.

He had to be in court on Friday morning, for the Potts divorce hearing. That only occupied an hour, and he was free at noon. He stopped at the nearest place for a quick sandwich, went back to the courthouse, and rode the elevator up to the county clerk's office. All he knew was the month and year; he couldn't tell the rather surly looking clerk the case number.

The clerk said he didn't know when he might locate the record. Jesse believed him; he'd had occasion to look up old cases before. Theoretically, a big-city bureau should maintain its records neatly and methodically filed; in practice, old records could get buried deep. It might take days to locate the transcript of that *State* versus *Richard Tredgold*, in which case he'd have to get the details of the case from the other Tredgolds, and he would rather read the gist in the impersonal transcript.

He told the clerk resignedly to call his office when the transcript was located and drove back to Hollywood.

But he was lucky, or the clerk more conscientious than he

looked. He got the call at three that afternoon and drove back downtown through a lessening drizzle of rain.

The transcript, of course, was on microfilm. He was given a rickety little table and chair in a square room full of mismatched file cabinets, and a hand projector. At least the fluorescent lighting was excellent. He bent over the little screen, taking occasional notes in his finicky copperplate.

It was a very simple story. Crime was seldom at all complicated, and of all crime homicide less apt to be.

The opening speech to the jury by the prosecuting deputy D.A. sketched out the plot.

". . . are concerned, ladies and gentlemen of the jury, with the death of Mrs. Louise Tredgold on August 16 of this year. I will give you, as briefly as possible, an account of what we will be presenting to you in sworn testimony concerning that death.

"The principals in this case are, as it happens, wealthy and educated people. Perhaps you may think that that fact makes this crime even more heinous than had it been a vulgar family brawl in some ghetto section of the city.

"Mrs. Tredgold, who was fifty-six, a widow, and the two nephews of her late husband, Walter and Richard Tredgold, were the sole owners of a large chain of supermarkets, and thus independently wealthy. Mrs. Tredgold had resided for a number of years in a large two-storied home in West Hollywood, on Sylvia Drive. You will hear testimony that although relations among them—Mrs. Tredgold, her older nephew Walter and his wife, her younger nephew Richard and his wife —had ordinarily been perfectly friendly, in the last few months prior to her death a quarrel had arisen. This quarrel was occasioned by Mrs. Tredgold's interest in a so-called psychic medium, Mrs. Sabrina Steele, and Mrs. Tredgold's avowed intention of presenting Mrs. Steele with a large sum of money in order to establish some sort of—er—spiritualistic center. There had been, as testimony will show, numerous heated arguments between Mrs. Tredgold and her two nephews on this subject. Both Walter and Richard Tredgold were convinced that their aunt was the victim of a confidence game. We will not be concerned with that, ladies and gentlemen; it is outside the scope of this enquiry, and I have mentioned it in passing only to explain to you the reason that this family dissension had arisen.

"On the day of the crime, which was a Friday, August 16, Mrs. Tredgold had been at home all day. Her automobile was in the garage for some necessary maintenance work and would not be returned to her until the following day. She was, however, planning to go out that evening, to dinner and the theater, with three women friends, who were to call for her around six-fifteen. Mrs. Tredgold employed, on a regular basis, a woman to help her with the general housework—Mrs. Jean Clark, who came to the house on the afternoons of Monday, Wednesday, and Friday. You will be hearing Mrs. Clark's testimony, which is very important in this case. On this particular day, Mrs. Clark had come to the house on Sylvia Drive at noon, and was there all afternoon.

"At approximately five o'clock that afternoon Mr. Richard Tredgold arrived at the house. Mrs. Clark let him in. According to her testimony, Mrs. Tredgold was then in her bedroom upstairs dressing for her evening out. Mrs. Clark called to her, informing her of Mr. Tredgold's arrival, and Mrs. Tredgold answered that she would come down, and that Mrs. Clark was to get what 'Mr. Dick' had come for. Mr. Tredgold's ostensible purpose in calling on his aunt was to pick up a punch bowl and set of cups which his wife wished to borrow for some social affair."

Jesse halted the projector there and reread that. The implication glossed over; he wondered if the defense attorney would have picked it up later for emphasis. Mrs. Alida Tredgold would undoubtedly have possessed her own punch bowl set; evidently the social affair was to include a few teetotalers, and she intended to provide spiked and unspiked punch. Or was that so obvious a deduction?

"Mrs. Clark therefore proceeded to the dining room where she obtained the punch bowl set, carried it to the kitchen and packed it in a box left ready, and took the box back to the front hall for Mr. Tredgold to take away. You will hear her tell you that at this time the door to the living room was closed, and that she could hear aunt and nephew in a heated argument, Mr. Tredgold's voice raised loudly. By reason of the door being closed, Mrs. Clark could not see whether Mrs. Tredgold was fully dressed for her evening party. This is an extremely important point which I must emphasize to you, for—to anticipate the chronological facts—when Mrs. Tredgold's body was found, she was fully dressed in a blue chiffon evening gown, which, all too evidently, she had been wearing when she was killed. Mr. Tredgold will tell you that when he talked with his aunt she was clad in a house robe, but we have, of course, only his word for this. On the other hand, Mrs. Clark, who had been employed by the deceased woman for almost a dozen years and knew her well, will tell you that it was Mrs. Tredgold's invariable habit to be dressed and ready for any engagement well ahead of time, and though she cannot swear to it she believes Mrs. Tredgold to have been fully dressed when she came downstairs to speak to her nephew.

"Mrs. Clark was due to leave at five-thirty, which she did. At this time, she will tell you, aunt and nephew were still in the living room, talking—Mr. Tredgold loudly. So she did not attempt to say good night to her employer, she simply went out the front door, got into her car, and drove away. The time is quite well established, independent of her evidence, since she stopped almost at once at a service station a few minutes' drive away, where the attendant will confirm her presence at approximately five thirty-five.

"Mrs. Richard Tredgold will tell you that her husband arrived home at ten minutes past six. But we are not dependent on her word for the time, since one of their neighbors also saw him arrive and confirms the time. The Richard Tredgolds were at this time living on Brinkley Road in Nichols Canyon in Hollywood, some twenty or thirty minutes' drive from the house on Sylvia Drive. Mr. Tredgold will tell you that he left his aunt, alive and well, immediately after five-thirty, and drove straight home. You may deduce that there is a discrepancy in time to be accounted for. I believe you have all been provided with a map of the relevant city area, and can judge for yourselves, by the distance involved, where any discrepancy may lie.

"At any rate, you will next hear from Mrs. Rena Werner, a resident of the same block on Sylvia Drive, that she was in her front yard doing some gardening work between the hours of four and six that afternoon—that she observed Mr. Tredgold arrive, Mrs. Clark leaving, and shortly afterward saw Mr. Tredgold leave—and that from then until six o'clock she can swear that not one other living soul passed up or down the block on either side.

"At ten minutes past six—early—Mrs. Tredgold's friends, with whom she was to pass the evening, arrived to pick her up. They are Mrs. Celia Adams, Mrs. Regina Moore, and Mrs. Agnes Decker. There was no answer to the doorbell, and finally they tried the door, and found it to be unlocked. They went in, to discover Mrs. Tredgold dead on the floor of the living room. You will hear the testimony of the doctor, who performed an autopsy, that she had been beaten to death, probably with the iron poker from the hearth set in the same room.

"I am sure the defense attorney will argue to you that it is conceivable that some casual thief entered the house, through that unlocked front door, between the time of Mr. Tredgold's departure and the arrival of these three women. That such a thief, unexpectedly confronted by the householder, panicked and struck her down. But, ladies and gentlemen, we must not forget the witness across the street, who can swear that no one at all stirred on that block between the time she saw Mr. Tredgold leave and the time she went into her own home. That leaves ten minutes—ten little minutes—for the casual thief to discover that unlocked door, venture in, strike down Mrs. Tredgold, and effect his escape. We will also show you evidence that all this while, the rear door of the house was securely locked, by Mrs. Clark before she left—and according to expert police evidence, no attempt had been made to break into the house at any point. Furthermore, Mr. and Mrs. Walter Tredgold will admit that there is nothing missing from the household."

Jesse thought that over for a minute, bent over the projector again, and discovered that that was about the end of what the prosecutor had to say for openers. He had wound up his speech neatly, promising to unfold the story for the jury in the witnesses' own words, and yielded the courtroom to Mr. Featherstone. The first paragraph of the defense attorney's opening rebuttal conjured up a graphic vision of him—probably, thought Jesse, all wrong—as a little fat fussy man, too fond of flowery oratory and inevitably boring to a jury.

After that ritual, the trial had got underway with the first prosecution witness, County Detective William McClure. He described his arrival on the scene at seven-ten, with County Detective Daniel Hoskins. "Mrs. Moore had called in, but she contacted the Hollywood L.A.P.D. station. They relayed it to us because West Hollywood's in our jurisdiction—that is, our territory. It's county territory. So there was a little delay. Two sheriff's deputies had got there at about a quarter to seven, and called back to the station reporting it a homicide, so I went out on it with Hoskins, and ordered a lab team to follow us out. We secured the scene for the lab men, and took the witnesses back to the station to talk to them.

Q. "To anticipate, Detective McClure, was any useful evidence obtained by the laboratory technicians—that is, fingerprints or anything like that?"

A. "No sir, there wasn't. Latent prints were picked up through the house which were identified as having been left by Mrs. Clark, Mr. Richard Tredgold, Mr. Walter Tredgold, and both the younger Mrs. Tredgolds, but we established that they'd often been in the house and those prints didn't have any significance. There were no other identifiable prints found in the house. It was impossible to get any prints from the rough iron of the poker."

Q. "Just tell the jury about the further police procedure in the case, if you will—what evidence led you to a possible suspect."

A. "Well, when we notified the family—that was at approximately eight-thirty—both Mr. Walter and Mr. Richard Tredgold showed up at the station, and Mr. Walter Tredgold was taken down to the morgue and formally identified the body. In talking with them, it came out that Mr. Richard Tredgold admitted leaving his aunt as late as five-thirty, and as we had already had an estimated time of death from the doctor—about that time to a quarter of six—we were interested in him right away. It didn't look as if she'd been attacked in the course of robbery, and later on Mr. and Mrs. Walter Tredgold confirmed that there was nothing missing from the house. It really turned out to be an open and shut case. The time was too tight for there to have been anyone else involved."

Q. "I will, of course, be calling for expert medical testimony, but just as we go along, what was the timetable of the crime as you deduced it from the evidence?"

A. "Well, it almost had to be that she was killed within five minutes of Mrs. Clark's leaving. Ten at the outside. We read it that Mr. Tredgold lost his temper in arguing with her, hit her with the poker, and rushed out of the house, possibly not even realizing that she was dead, though nobody'll ever know about that. And—"

At this point the clerk tapped Jesse's shoulder and said tersely, "Building's closing." It was five o'clock. Jesse swore. And the weekend intervening— But he had the bare bones of the thing, and a very tight little case it looked. "Don't hide this away again," he said, "I'm not finished with it." He watched the clerk staple a card with his name onto the box of microfilm before he left. At least it had stopped raining.

At home, Nell eyed him and asked no questions; when his interest was roused on something he liked to mull it over to himself awhile. Philosophically she went into the study after dinner, found a book, and left him alone.

———————————

Saturday morning, earlier than he usually got out and about on a weekend, found Jesse heading for Sergeant Clock's office. The Hollywood precinct had finally, this last six months, been given a brand-new headquarters, around on Fountain from the tired old tan brick precinct building on Wilcox. It was a handsome white stucco building, more spacious than the old one, occupying the whole block on Fountain between Cole and Wilcox.

Jesse walked in the front door past the strip of green lawn and red brick planters outside, and down the long corridor past the desk sergeant, turned left down a short hall with double doors at its end, and wandered into the detective squad room. Unlike the old one, with its scarred wooden floor, old double-hung windows, ancient golden oak desks, this spacious tall-windowed room had a smart vinyl-tile floor, metal Venetian blinds, modern steel desks. The fluorescent bars over each desk poured soft brilliance, shadowless.

A man at the other side of the room was typing a report. Clock was sitting at his desk reading what looked like a letter, and Detective Petrovsky was immersed in a paperback at the next desk.

"Like an opinion off the record, Andrew," said Jesse, perching one hip on the corner of Clock's desk. Clock looked up at him a little vaguely, massaging his prognathous jaw in habitual gesture.

"About what?"

"Cops," said Jesse. "I'm looking at a homicide case eight years old—never mind why—and it was investigated by the sheriff's department. They as efficient as the old reliable L.A.P.D.? Apt to overlook things, get a little careless?"

Clock laughed. "Maybe you're asking the wrong man. We all know the L.A.P.D. is the top force anywhere. When the requirements and standards are so high, it just naturally gets a higher quality of men. But the sheriff's boys are all right. Almost any big police department—and that one's bigger than us —with the kind of funding they've got, is bound to be reasonably efficient. I think you can take it they wouldn't make any boo-boos looking at a homicide. Why? You playing detective again?"

"I don't know," said Jesse. "Don't know there's any detecting to do. Whole case dead as a doornail—where the hell could you look, after all this time? I just thought I'd ask." He stood up and stretched. "You're looking a trifle harried—keeping busy?"

Petrovsky looked up from his book. "He's misplaced a body, and it's making him nervous. I say let it lay, a suicide's bound to turn up sometime. Suicide we know it was, he left a note."

"But where the hell did he go?" demanded Clock. "Where in hell could he kill himself and disappear in the middle of the city? It doesn't make sense."

"He'll turn up sometime," repeated Petrovsky. "Just be thankful there's no weeping relatives on our necks."

"I've read that damned note over a hundred times and it still doesn't make sense." The phone on Clock's desk buzzed and he picked it up. "Yeah, Dan? O.K.—what's the address?" He scrawled on his desk pad. "Come on, Pete, no rest for the wicked. We've got another homicide."

Jesse followed them out. He sat in the Mercedes for five minutes staring into space, finally started the engine, drove down Fountain to Cahuenga, down that to Santa Monica, turned right there and went up seven blocks to DeWitt's lair on the second floor of an old office building.

He found DeWitt discussing filing systems with Miss Duffy in the first of their four rooms where the file cases were accumulating. "Morning, Jesse. What did you think of that tape?" DeWitt hadn't been in when Jesse had dropped it off on Wednesday morning.

"Oh, very interesting. Do you know anything about a supposed medium by the name of Sabrina Steele?"

DeWitt looked blank. "Never heard of her. Why?"

"Oh, excuse me, Mr. Falkenstein, I have," said Miss Duffy.

"I don't know anything about her, but"—she looked a little embarrassed—"there were just a couple of lines mentioning her in a sort of social-gossip column in the *Star* the other day."

"Why on earth were you reading that?" asked DeWitt, astonished.

"There wasn't anything else but film magazines and worse at the beauty salon," said Miss Duffy, "and I'd left my book in the car. By the little it said, the Steele woman has quite a following here. It called her a 'fashionable psychic'—I don't know what in the world that's supposed to mean."

"Clients with money, probably," said Jesse. "Don't like her name much—a little too good to be true. Is there any way to get her address?"

"Now what's in your mind?" asked DeWitt.

"Nothing to do with you, but I may as well use your letterhead. What about it, Miss Duffy?"

"If she's on the make," said Miss Duffy ironically, "she won't have an unlisted number." She flipped open the Los Angeles book, didn't find a listing, tried Hollywood and said, "Here you are. Melrose in West Hollywood."

"Good. How'd you like to write her a letter, William. Tell her anything—you're looking for gifted psychics to help your research, or whatever. Invite her to look over your projects."

"And what am I supposed to do with her if she comes? I may be prejudiced," said DeWitt. "I don't know anything about the woman, she may be another Estelle Roberts, but I somehow doubt it."

"I don't think she will," said Jesse. "I'd just like to know more about her."

That afternoon he went to see the Tredgolds.

━━━━━◆━━━━━

They looked at him incredulously when he told them what Dick Tredgold had said. "Out of his mind," said Walt tiredly. "That's crazy." After a minute he lit the cigarette he'd been turning round and round in his fingers.

"Been looking over the trial transcript," said Jesse. "Very simple little case, as far as I've got."

"Wasn't it?" said Walt. "Look, Mr. Falkenstein. That's ridiculous, as Dick would know if he was thinking straight. When no other evidence turned up at the time—I'm aware that the police here are pretty damned efficient. If you've read the gist of the evidence, you can see how it looked. The time was so tight. We all wracked our brains to think what could have happened, who could have—but there was just nothing. The police were naturally led to Dick right away. And all he had was his bare word that he'd left her alive. I will say, I think the police didn't look any further because they were so sure he did it—but would there have been any more evidence to find if they'd looked? My private eyes didn't turn up anything at all."

"What agency was it?" This was a very expectable house for the Tredgolds to live in: not old, not new, a big stucco house on a double lot, on a quiet residential street in Santa Monica. The living room was furnished in good Early American, quiet colors. There was one good seascape, some flower prints. A glimpse into a formal dining room across the central hall showed conventional dining furniture in walnut. They didn't throw money around on showy things, but it all said comfort and good taste. He couldn't see from the street, but there was probably a pool in the back yard.

"Wheelock and Ellis," said Walt.

"Good enough firm. I suppose you didn't get them on it until your brother'd been arrested?"

"Oh, they were already working for me. I'd had them following up that Steele woman."

"Oh," said Jesse. "Yes, I see."

"I thought if I could show Aunt Lou some definite evidence that the woman was a fraud—but they hadn't come up with anything. I still don't understand how Aunt Lou could have fallen for a con game like that. She'd never been interested in all that guff."

"No? Lot of women are. What your brother said about her—Billie Burke type? A little frivolous—"

"Oh no," said Becky Tredgold. She'd been sitting quietly on the couch listening, and spoke up suddenly. "She gave that impression, I suppose you could say—ingenuous, is that the word? She certainly wasn't any intellectual—I never knew her to read a book—just women's magazines, sometimes. But she wasn't silly, Mr. Falkenstein. She was a—a nice woman."

Walt said slowly, "I suppose Dick might forget it, because by the time he was noticing things all the money had built up, Aunt Lou was just—enjoying life. But at the first, she'd worked right along with Uncle Walt, in their first market—checkout clerk, and later on in the office. She wasn't a fool by any means. That's why we couldn't understand her falling so hard for the psychic bit. But the private eyes hadn't found out much about the Steele woman up to—"

"At least," said Becky, "they listened, about that diamond brooch. Which was more than the police did. I never felt so charitable toward the police as you—"

"For God's sake, I didn't feel exactly—"

"They just saw that Dick could have done it, and decided he probably did, so they didn't bother to look any further." She sounded tart. They had probably not discussed this for years, a dead hurt in the past, and now it had come alive again.

"What about a diamond brooch?" asked Jesse gently.

"Well, it never turned up, you know," said Becky. "They asked us to look through the house and say if anything was missing. And nothing was, that we could see. Walt had identified her body, and he said she had on the blue chiffon evening dress. She had a good deal of jewelry, you see, but I was familiar with all of it, and nothing was gone—except the rings she always wore, the diamond and sapphire one, and her wedding and engagement rings—and that brooch. It was a plain round brooch with eight big diamonds in a circle, four carats of diamonds."

"Uncle Walt was always giving her jewelry," said Tredgold absently. "He thought diamonds were a good investment."

"And she wore it a good deal, that brooch I mean, when she was dressed up. Always with that evening dress. So I assumed it was—on her body, and we'd get it back eventually. I didn't mention it to the police. What I did tell them, they didn't pay any attention to. All that finagling and arguing about how she was dressed— Dick said she had on a housecoat when he saw her, and I'm positive she was all dressed underneath and just ready to put on her dress. Because when I was in her bedroom —that was the next day, and the police said nothing had been moved—there was her diamond and sapphire bracelet, and the sapphire earrings, and her good watch, all laid out on the dressing table. She always put jewelry away when she took it off. So I know exactly what did happen," said Becky calmly. "After Dick left, she went back upstairs and put on her dress. Hung up the housecoat. And she was just starting to put on her jewelry, when—something happened."

"Interesting," said Jesse. "The brooch never showed up?"

"When they released the body, we got her rings back from the coroner's office, but they claimed she hadn't been wearing any other jewelry. And we told the police about that, but they couldn't have been less interested. They'd already arrested Dick, and they couldn't have cared less."

Walt said abruptly, "Look here, you're not really thinking of delving into all this again? It's a wild goose chase."

"Bound to say, it looks like a waste of time," agreed Jesse. "But once in a while—like your wife—I get a feeling. Inclined to think your brother was innocent, all right. What about the punch bowl set, by the way?"

They looked taken aback. "What about it?" asked Becky.

"Did he bring it home with him?"

"Well, of course."

"Of course. What he'd come to get. And the run of the mill crimes cops look at year in, year out, don't tend to exercise the imagination. I really do think Andrew'd have seen that, but maybe Detective McClure, despite his Celtic name, hasn't any imagination. I mean, you know, you can't have it both ways."

"What do you mean?" asked Becky.

"Well, the Clark woman left the punch bowl set packed in a

box in the front hall. She didn't carry it out to his car. And if it happened the way they tried to make out, he lost his temper and started a slanging match with your aunt, ended by grabbing the poker and killing her, it's a hundred to one he'd have forgotten all about that punch bowl set. He'd probably have rushed out in a blind panic to get away. And on the other hand, if he'd only pretended to lose his temper, meant to kill her—which is damned farfetched—he'd hardly have started that loud argument while the maid was still there."

"That's funny, I never thought of that," said Walt. "But you're right, sure. That's another thing—that made it all so—so unreal. About all the arguments. The way they made it sound—sure, we'd both had arguments with her, but not to the extent they made out. We were—more impatient with her, for falling for this idiotic stuff, trying to make her see how silly it was. After all, it was her money—we just didn't like to see her throwing it away. Neither Dick nor I felt so strongly about it that we'd have got that mad at her— That was just ridiculous, to think he'd lose his temper that far over a thing like that."

"And nobody, of course, ever listened to me except Alida," said Becky, "but I always suspected Jean Clark. She's a sneaking malicious woman. I don't know how Aunt Lou stood her, or anybody else—she worked for several other people on that block. About half the block had the same gardener too, not that that says anything—he wasn't there that day, he did Aunt Lou's yard on Thursdays, I think. But the Clark woman— I'm perfectly sure she stole that other brooch, the ruby one. She convinced Aunt Lou it'd been left on a dress sent to the cleaners, but I'd swear she took it."

"Slander, Mrs. Tredgold," said Jesse. "By the times, she couldn't have done the murder if she'd had a reason to."

"How do we know? She says she left before Dick, but what's to say she didn't come back? All this quibbling about times— you never know the exact minute, watches vary so. That woman across the street could have gone in the house at ten to six or even before. Aunt Lou's girl friends could have come by ten minutes later than they said. That Clark woman was a sneak. She could have come back, and Aunt Lou caught her stealing something."

Walt just shook his head. "I wonder whether she's still working around there," said Jesse. "The three girl friends still around?"

"Heavens, I don't know—I suppose so. They were all about her age. I think we had a Christmas card from Mrs. Moore last year. They all lived in that area—Mrs. Moore in Hollywood."

"I suppose," said Jesse, "the house was sold."

"That's right. That was lucky," said Walt, "if anything about it was lucky. If it had been hers to will away, it'd have been tied up until the legal tangle over the will was settled. But it was part of the trust. Uncle Walt loved that house—it was the first and only house they owned, and I think he was afraid Aunt Lou might decide to move to a flashy new apartment and sell the family mansion to strangers. It was too big for her—"

"She'd have been better off in an apartment," said Becky. "And she wouldn't have needed the Clark woman to help with the housework. It was a lovely house, but far too big, of course. We sold it as soon as we could. Oddly enough, some people who lived across the street bought it, people named Walsh. He was a stockbroker or something. They bought some of the furniture too."

"We can't expect you to waste your time on this, Mr. Falkenstein," said Tredgold formally. "I think Dick's out of his mind."

Jesse rose from the armchair. "Sometimes," he said, "you find useful little ideas in unexpected places. Detective stories, for instance. Remember reading one once—forget what or who by, or was it Christie? or Carr?—a theory that sometimes it's easier to get at the truth of a thing a while after it's happened. When you can get a perspective on it. Don't know how much there might be to it, outside fiction. But it's an interesting idea." He grinned at Walt. "Don't worry about my making a lot of busywork and handing you a four-figure bill. I'm feeling sort of curious about this. I can afford to neglect the office some when I feel like it. I'd just like to poke around on it a little."

"Well, we're not asking you to," said Walt heavily. "I guess we just let Dick go on being a damn fool. But thanks for trying anyway."

"Sure," said Jesse casually. They came to the door with him politely. As he went down the front walk, a station wagon pulled up at the curb and a couple of kids got out of it—a teen-aged boy and girl, both dark, nice-looking. They scampered past him with hardly a look. It had begun to drizzle again.

He started feeling cautious about Andrew's opinion of the sheriff's boys at Valley Station. The desk sergeant didn't seem to like him much, or the detective he finally summoned to deal with him. Prejudices, Jesse reminded himself, cut both ways; these days, cops in general might not much like any lawyer, having too often seen the slick tricks get the street criminals off with a slap on the wrist. He was patient and polite.

"Listen, McClure retired last year," said the detective, who was medium black, with a mustache and cold eyes. "What's it about?"

"A case he worked on," said Jesse. "I just want to talk to him. Doesn't anybody know where he's retired to?"

"Oh, hell. Maybe Holst might know, they always hung together. I guess he's someplace around, I'll look." Ten minutes later the black detective came back and handed Jesse a slip of paper with an address in Glendale scrawled on it.

It was raining harder.

The address in Glendale was a pink stucco house on a narrow curving street opposite a big public-school playground. A thin gray-haired woman in shabby slacks and sweater let him in, took him down to a small dark-paneled room furnished as a den. But the little desk was bare, the few books undusted, and the man there was sitting watching an old movie on a portable TV, a can of beer in one hand.

He turned the TV down grudgingly; he listened to Jesse and grunted. He was a big man running to fat, with a bald head and a hard voice.

"Look," he said, "do you know how many cases I handled in twenty-eight years on the force? Thousands! I'm supposed to remember any details, on a case eight years back?"

"Not that many homicides," said Jesse. "Should think you'd remember something. Wealthy family, aunt and two nephews. Tredgold. West Hollywood."

McClure pondered. "Yeah, I do remember something about it. Nothing to work, as it comes back to me. Showed up right off who'd done it—one of the nephews."

"You didn't have any doubts about it? Any other suspect?"

"Not that I recall. It's a little vague." McClure shrugged. "Open and shut. There'd been some kind of family fight about money—they were loaded."

"Do you remember that after the rest of the family had told you there was nothing missing from the house, they came back and told you there was a piece of jewelry missing—a diamond brooch they'd thought was on the body, only the coroner's office said it wasn't?"

McClure finished the beer and set the can down with a little clatter. "Did they? Yeah, I do sort of call it to mind."

"Apparently you didn't think it was important—you didn't go looking, ask any questions."

McClure looked at him sourly. "I do remember that place now, sort of. Far as I recall, I didn't see how they could be sure, one piece of jewelry—she had a houseful. I do remember we made the arrest pretty quick, on that one. Two, three days after the kill. The case was out of our hands, and it wasn't worth following up."

"You didn't consider it a little new evidence to follow up?"

"Why? Probably not, if we didn't look at it. Also, probably a dozen other things had come up in the meantime. We always got kept busy." McClure chuckled reminiscently and belched. "Yeah, I do remember about that now. Listen, for God's sake, you don't say things right out to the civilians, but I seem to recall saying to Holst, about that—hell, they don't pay the morgue attendants all that high, and it could have been one of the corpse washers grabbed off whatever was on the corpse.

That's all I remember about it, hadn't thought of it from that day to this."

"I see," said Jesse. "Thanks very much."

McClure shrugged. "These days, you better believe I'm glad to be out of the rat race."

Heading back for Hollywood, Jesse reflected that that had been a little waste of time; and if he couldn't wholly agree with Andrew's opinion of the sheriff's boys, he'd ask him what he thought about the incorruptibility of the coroner's office. It was pouring a torrent as he came in the back door of the house to find Nell inspecting a roast in the oven, with Athelstane hovering hopefully.

"Good day, darling?"

"Not specially," said Jesse. "I really don't know where I am on this thing, or where to look. There is, of course, Wheelock. And Sabrina. Lovely name. But if Sabrina was expecting fifty grand from Aunt Lou—which is rather funny—several funny things—I don't suppose she'd have had a reason— Though there isn't usually much reason about homicide, of course. However—"

"You're not making much sense," said Nell. "Dinner in twenty minutes, if you want a drink first."

"I think I need one."

He had run across Harry Wheelock of that private detective agency a couple of times in court, and after dinner he took a chance calling the office number. Like the police, private detectives worked all hours. Athelstane sat lovingly on his feet, interested in the peculiar noises inside the phone.

Wheelock was friendly. "Sure I remember you. That thing," he said when he heard the Tredgold name. "I remember it, some, and I've got files. Nothing ever gets tossed out here, someday we'll have to get bigger offices to accommodate all the paperwork. Look, I've got to be in the office tomorrow morning. If you could drop by, say ten o'clock, I can probably give you what we got on it."

THREE

The Wheelock and Ellis office was far down Vermont. At least on Sunday there were plenty of parking slots on the street, with the meters not working. The premises weren't fancy; Jesse climbed dusty uncarpeted stairs to the third floor and found the door with the right sign unlocked, went into a small square anteroom with an untenanted desk. Wheelock appeared in a door opening to the right.

"You've lost me a morning's work," he said. He was a big egg-shaped man with a bulldog face. Jesse had once heard him give evidence in a damage suit and was aware that he was an ex-L.A.P.D. sergeant, invalided out of the force after getting shot by a sniper. "What's the idea of raking up this old business?"

Jesse thought he might be interested and told him. He snorted incredulously. "You don't really expect to find anything new? That is one for the books. Come in, sit down. I looked up the reports for you, and got interested, looking them over. Wasted the morning."

"You remember much about it?"

"Sure. The reports brought it back. Private eyes don't often get mixed up in homicide cases—of course it didn't start out that way. For what it's worth, which is damn all, I didn't think Tredgold was guilty."

"Neither do I, but I couldn't exactly say why." This other office was long and narrow, cluttered with two desks, file cases, a typewriter on a metal stand.

"Well, I could," said Wheelock flatly. "You're familiar with the details? All right. I can see—as an ex-cop—why they dropped on him right off the bat. Quite literally there wasn't anybody else. But I don't think the sheriff's boys thought it out far enough—or the D.A.'s office, come to that. Because I gave it some dry runs, and I don't think he'd possibly have had time to kill her."

"You mean—"

"I mean, Dick Tredgold getting home to Brinkley Road from Sylvia Drive, and getting there when he did. At five-thirty on a Friday afternoon—when he started out, that is. That particular day. I asked his brother about his route, but of course there wasn't much choice. He went up San Vicente to Sunset and up the Strip, turned up to Hollywood Boulevard and then onto Nichols Canyon Road, up to Brinkley. At that hour, everybody getting away from offices a little early on Friday, the traffic'd be murder. You know the Strip." That curving section of Sunset was old and narrow, with parking both sides, and usually slow going. "And there was some repair work going on along a couple of blocks on San Vicente, only two lanes open. I tried a dry run three times"—Wheelock tapped the thick Manila folder on his blotter—"results in here. The best I did was forty-six minutes, and that was starting just before five-thirty."

"Now that aspect hadn't struck me," said Jesse thoughtfully.

"If he did kill the woman, it must have taken him at least three or four minutes," said Wheelock. "Even if he started bashing her just after the Clark woman left the house, he couldn't very well have left himself much before five thirty-five or even a few minutes later. And he was seen arriving home by the next-door neighbor at ten past six. It just looked too tight to me."

"Yes," said Jesse, "and at the same time—"

"Oh, it was *possible*," said Wheelock. "Don't fault the county boys, Falkenstein—they're efficient cops. He was the only suspect, standing out like a sore thumb, and when the D.A.'s office looked at the evidence they decided they could make the charge stick. Strict legal justice doesn't always work out by the book. Nuances."

"Meaning?"

Wheelock was peeling a fat cigar. "I was at the trial, you

know. Interested to see what might come out. Not much did. The bare facts of the case, and—I don't know"—he rubbed his bulbous nose—"it always seems to me, things get distorted a little, brought out all formal in legal talk. His attorney wasn't much damn good to Tredgold. And he—Tredgold—made a bad impression on the stand."

"How?"

Wheelock snipped the end off the cigar, lit it, and sat back in the old-fashioned golden-oak desk chair, contemplating the burning tip of the cigar. "I've seen that kind of thing happen before, and I expect you've seen more of it. He was probably scared to death—young fellow with his background, enough money, suddenly put through all that, police questioning, murder charge, jail—no bail on a homicide charge, of course— and then the trial. He hadn't been married long, his wife was expecting a baby. Pretty little thing she was, blond with big green eyes."

"She lost the baby. She was killed a year later, driving up to visit him in prison."

Wheelock said quietly. "That's a bastard. I didn't know that. Very tough indeed. But what I was going to say, he was trying to sound assured, self-confident, answering all the questions straightforward, and he overdid it. He came out sounding either arrogant or indifferent."

"I can see how he might have," said Jesse. He thought back to Dick Tredgold, the regular-featured, good-looking smooth face, the slightly mocking voice. Eight years ago, Tredgold would have been less experienced, less assured, at first disbelieving it was happening to him, assuming a desperate overconfidence.

"I think that turned the trick. The jury read him as a spoiled rich boy losing his temper. Juries can be funny."

"You're telling me?" said Jesse. "Walt Tredgold had sicked you onto the Steele woman to start with."

"That's right. We couldn't get anything on her at all. They might have just come down from Mars. I don't even know that they'd just landed here, though I suspect it. There's a supposed husband, Rodney—it was a nice genteel front, he was supposed to be a retired professor doing research on a book. She's a slick piece of goods—"

"You don't think she was the genuine article?"

"I do not," said Wheelock, rolling the cigar around his mouth. "Don't know much about that, but I guess now and then you get somebody with real what d'youcallit—ESP. I don't think she's one of 'em. But as I told Tredgold, I'd be committing slander to say they were on the con—I couldn't prove it. I went so far as to attend one of the meetings." Wheelock laughed shortly. "They were living in a cheap rented bungalow on a side street off Fountain, pretty sleazy. One room fixed up as a kind of chapel. You know the city rules about fortune-tellers—they get round it by having the mail-order diplomas as ministers of the far-out sects. There it was, framed on the wall."

"Spiritualist church?" It so often was. And of course that genuine religion hadn't policed its own ranks the way it should, in this country at least.

"No—something called Spiritual Brotherhood. I can't say she impressed me," said Wheelock with a grin. "I didn't get any messages from the dear departed. But as far as either that or the homicide went, we got nothing. There wasn't anywhere to look, on the murder—that amiable soft comfortable lady Louise Tredgold, how she struck me, ambling along through life, nobody even disliked her, she hadn't any business winding up murdered. And I don't think Tredgold did it, but I am damned if I could get any faint smell as to who did, or how it was done."

"You couldn't come up with anything on Steele at all?"

"For what it's worth, neither of them had a record. You needn't ask how we got their prints, or why an old pal of mine downtown at headquarters passed them to NCIC. They weren't known anywhere."

"You're a fount of information." Jesse rose from the chair. "I really don't know why I'm wasting time like this. The damned case is—was—a handful of nothing."

"It wasn't much more at the time," said Wheelock. "Now it's even less."

"What about the Clark woman? Mrs. Tredgold didn't like her. You look at her close?"

"We did—we were getting paid to look, after the arrest. I can't say I liked her either, but there was nothing against her. She'd worked for Mrs. Tredgold eleven years or so, also a couple of other women in the neighborhood. Everybody said she was a good worker, and reliable. At the time she was forty-three, divorced, had a couple of teen-age daughters. Lived in a rented house on Berendo."

"Um," said Jesse. "I'll take the address. I don't suppose she'll still be there."

"Persistent, are you, or just too dumb to know you're hunting thin air?"

"Somebody killed the woman for some reason," said Jesse, "and neither of us thinks it was Tredgold."

"Which doesn't say it wasn't," said Wheelock. "I've been wrong before now and I guess you have too."

"There is that. But there are always things that don't come out in a trial—irrelevancies that don't seem to matter at the time. Looking back at a thing with more perspective, well, things like that might not look so irrelevant."

"If that means anything, I don't know what it is."

"I'm not sure I do," said Jesse.

At least Wheelock could give him addresses, though how many of them would be valid after eight years was another thing. Curiously, he didn't especially want to see Jean Clark until he'd finished looking at the trial transcript. Mrs. Regina Moore had been living at an address in Hollywood, Romaine Street. It was a large old apartment building, and her name was on one of the mailboxes in the lobby. He got no answer at the third-floor apartment. It was the kind of place where a manageress lived on the premises; he tried that door and a stout red-haired woman in a pink housecoat opened it promptly.

"Mis' Moore? She's on vacation, won't be back for the next week," she informed him. She looked at his card with interest. "Lawyer, you are? Somebody left her some money, maybe? God knows she could use some, couldn't we all. Well, she'll be back a week from tomorrow."

The next address Wheelock had written down for him happened to be that of Celia Adams. Glasgow Road. When he found it, it was just over the county line from West Hollywood, into Hollywood proper. It was a single house, not very big, on a modest block of older homes; it had a little lawn in front, a big rounded picture window, and it was painted white with green trim: very conventional.

He was vaguely surprised. Romaine Street; this place. Little connection with Sylvia Drive.

The woman who opened the door was in her sixties, little and trim and once very pretty. The moment she opened her mouth Jesse thought that here was the real Billie Burke type. A nice woman, a little silly, a little shallow, perennially girlish. She was doubtful of him at first.

"But why should a lawyer be asking questions about that, all this time after?"

"Well, you know, the family always felt there were things that didn't come out at the time. And it was an interesting case —er, legally speaking—that is, to a lawyer, even now. The Tredgolds—"

"Oh, you're working for the family, some way?"

"Mrs. Walter Tredgold was sure you'd try to be helpful," said Jesse persuasively.

"Well, goodness, I don't see—but I guess any way I can help —they're very nice people, of course. I don't understand what you're after, but I suppose you can come in, Mr."—she looked at the card—"Mr. Falkenstein. My husband isn't here, he's out bowling, but I don't suppose you want to see him anyway."

It was a modest middle-class living room, rather shabby old furniture, worn carpet, everything neat and clean but never expensive. He was surprised again, thinking about Aunt Lou and her diamonds. She asked him to sit down and perched on a rocker opposite him, looking at him curiously with bright brown eyes. Her neat figure was modish in a black-and-white-checked pantsuit, and the silver-gray curls on her forehead exquisitely arranged.

And as he'd suspected, once he got her talking she went on in spate, like Tennyson's brook. After a few questions he hit on the right one. "Had you known Mrs. Tredgold long, Mrs. Adams?"

It all began to come out, in greater detail as she settled to the pleasure of reminiscence. Oh, she and Lou had known each other forever, they'd been in school together, and Regina to, of course, they'd all graduated from Fairfax High. Each other's closest friends. Sometimes old friends grew away from each other, but they never had, and old friends were best— "Even though things turned out different for all of us, and Lou was so lucky, her husband made a lot of money, all those markets, but she never let it make any difference, it didn't change her at all, except that she *had* things, you know, that beautiful house, all the jewelry, and so on. But she didn't have any children, she was unlucky there—of course neither did Regina, she was the really unlucky one, poor Regina, getting divorced so soon and she's had to work all her life, she was a secretary at Monsanto. Of course I've always had things pretty easy, Rex always made decent money, he's in construction, and we had four children. Lou was so pleased when she and Walt took the two boys, such nice boys she always said, and then to think what happened—it was the most terrible time I ever went through—finding her like that, all the blood—to think one of them did that to her—"

Jesse opened his mouth, too slowly.

"Of course Lou wasn't ever very social-minded, she didn't entertain much. When he was alive her husband was all business, and Rex isn't one for going out—not as if we went around in couples, even when Regina was still married—but we liked to get together, just all girls, once in a while—it was like that, you see, that night we were going out. And the really terrible thing is that I felt it was at least partly my fault, you know. Because what came out, it was all over that money Lou was going to give Madame Sabrina. Oh, she always says not to say madame, but it seems natural to call her that—because I was the one who took Lou there first. She didn't want to come, she said she wasn't interested, but it was all so impressive—you know, Mr. Falkenstein, she was able to bring my darling boy back to me, my little boy I lost when he was only three, and he knew me at once, and called me Mama just as he used to. And you see, Lou never did go to church, and I just somehow felt she needed this wonderful reassurance that it isn't all for nothing, everyone we've loved is waiting on the other side and another beautiful life waiting too. And finally I got her to come to one of the public sittings—Sabrina wasn't charging as much for private sittings then, but I couldn't afford those—you see, it's the terrible drain on her system, she can't hold many sittings, it would be too hard on her health, and her spirit guides had explained carefully that we must take care of her, she has such a wonderful psychic gift. Just as the Bible says, the laborer worthy of his hire. And just as I knew would happen, Lou was terribly impressed. Nothing really came through for her the first time, but I was sure it would, and sure enough, the second time she went her husband came through just splendidly, he called her by name and gave all sorts of proof he was really there, told her a lot of things nobody else could possibly have known, and asked about the boys and all sorts of things, and it was a real revelation to her. She'd never known about all these psychic things, the astral world and all that, and she was terribly interested. Of course it was different with Regina, we couldn't even talk to her about it, she thinks it's all nonsense—if she would only open her mind and heart, as Lou did—

"But you can see how terrible I felt about it, when that awful thing happened. All because she had got interested, and wanted to give Madame Sabrina some money, for the Spiritual Brotherhood Foundation. Of course it's *there* now, because the money came from somewhere and they could buy the building. But that was why that awful young man killed Lou, just the money. And another thing," Celia Adams sniffed and blinked, "to think it happened just then, when she was so happy—she was going to be married again—"

"What?" said Jesse, startled.

"Oh, dear," she said, and fished a handkerchief out of her pocket and blew her nose. "Oh, *dear*, you said you were from the family. And she hadn't told them—she didn't really tell me anything, or Regina either, just enough so we guessed. Well, I don't suppose it matters now, all this time after."

"What exactly did she tell you? When?" asked Jesse.

"Oh, not much at all. She just said, now let me think, it was when we went to see the new Disney movie, that was about three weeks before—before she died—she picked me up, we took her car that night, and she was acting so young and happy, she looked so pretty. She said don't be surprised if I have some interesting news before long, and I said did she mean she had a boy friend—joking, you know—and she laughed and said what else. Of course I was dying to hear more, but she just said wait and see and there wasn't anything settled yet. Regina wasn't with us, and as soon as I could I called her and asked if she knew anything, but she didn't, she was awfully surprised too. She said she just hoped Lou knew what she was doing, it could be some con man after her money, but she always looks on the dark side. Lou was still terribly attractive, you know, she kept her hair touched up and of course she could buy the most beautiful clothes. And—"

"She didn't mention any name?" asked Jesse loudly.

"Oh no. The last time I talked to her—oh, dear, it was that morning, I called to tell her when we'd pick her up, Regina was taking her car, we were going out to dinner and on to see *Blithe Spirit*—and I said, when were we going to hear about the boy friend, and she laughed and said maybe soon, and then she got serious and said she was a little nervous about telling the family and I wasn't to say a word—not that I ever saw the Tredgolds anyway. Of course I said I understood."

"Did she mention where she'd met him, anything about him at all?"

"No, she didn't. But she seemed so happy about it. It just seemed such a *waste*, she was only fifty-six. One thing she did say then was that she felt it was going to be all right, because Walter hadn't said a word to her about it. Her husband, you know. He usually came through to her at sittings. And of course he'd know about it, on the other side, and he hadn't mentioned it at all, and she felt if it wasn't right for her he'd have warned her, so she felt it was all right."

Marveling slightly at female logic, Jesse asked, "How did you—um—get in touch with Madame Sabrina in the first place?"

"Oh, it was Wilma, Wilma Pangborn, she works at the place I get my hair done, and it was about four months before, she pointed out this column in the paper when I was there, it was a sort of society column in the Hollywood *News*, and the woman—it was a woman who wrote it—said what a gifted psychic Mrs. Sabrina Steele was, and she was giving public sittings, and the address. So I thought I'd go. I've always been interested in all that, but I didn't know there were any mediums right around here. And really, it quite changed my life, so terribly reassuring to know nobody dies really, and they can come back and speak with us. In a way, I'm just glad Lou knew that too, before she went." She gave a final sniff into the handkerchief and the bright brown eyes were a little vague on him. "I still don't know why you'd be interested in all this."

And where that might lead he couldn't see; but it was certainly something new. Maybe he'd been using ESP himself when he said new facts might emerge with time passed. But how to track down the elusive boy friend—when she'd been that discreet with an old, close friend, and never a word to the family, it wasn't likely that anybody knew anything more. Still, she must have had other friends—possibly she'd been less discreet with somebody. But why in hell hadn't the boy friend shown up at the time? At least come forward to express condolences?

But postulate any wild possibility you wanted: say the boy friend disapproved of Sabrina and was about to deprive her of one good paying client—say Sabrina was getting impatient for the promised fifty G's—say Jean Clark had a boy friend who was a pro burglar and she cased the place for him, and how wild could you get—you still came back to that forty-five minutes' tight time, to the empty block in late afternoon of an August day, to the locked rear door. To, when you came to think of it, a locked-room puzzle.

Jesse went home, stacked "The Art of the Fugue" on the new stereo, and stretched out on the couch. Nell had left a note; she was out looking at houses.

He didn't go into the office on Monday morning, but called in. He told Jimmy not to take any appointments for a while. He was at the courthouse when it opened, and a different clerk only took forty minutes to find the box of microfilm the other one had stashed away. This time Jesse had had the foresight to bring an ashtray.

There wasn't much more of McClure. At the end of his session, he was talking about the security of that rear door. "There was a screen door, it wasn't hooked, but the inside wooden door was locked. It's a Yale lock with a dead bolt. The same key fit the front and back doors, and we found Mrs. Tredgold's keys in her purse upstairs. The only other set of keys to the house belonged to Mr. Walter Tredgold, in case of emergency. We found a screen loose on the window in the service porch, but that was explained when Mrs. Clark told us she'd been washing windows that afternoon, and evidently forgot to hook the screen after she replaced it. Anyway, the window was only about two feet square, and there were no signs of entry."

Exit McClure. Then, of course, the medical evidence. The surgeon hadn't much to offer. Since they knew she'd been alive at five-thirty and dead at six-ten, all he could say was that she'd died between those times, no way to pin it down tighter.

Q. "Would you describe to the court the actual injuries sustained by the deceased and the cause of death, Doctor."

A. "Well, there were three blows struck, quite certainly with the poker found beside her—there was her blood and hair on it. The cause of death was simple fracture of the skull, to the left temple area. I don't suppose I need to use technical terms obscure to the jury. That was almost certainly the first blow, and it seems to have been purely accidental, if I may put it that way, that it was a fatal blow—just bad luck it landed where it did. There was certainly no anatomical knowledge shown. She fell to the floor then, and while she was on the floor two more blows were struck, causing facial injuries, damage to one eye—the right—and causing copious bleeding from the nose and eye."

Q. "Would it have taken an inordinate amount of strength to cause such injuries with that weapon?"

A. "Not excessive strength, no. In fact, not much strength at all. The poker is good solid iron, weighing nearly four pounds. The deceased was not a large woman—five foot two, a hundred and ten pounds. The weight of the poker alone would have augmented quite a small amount of physical strength."

Q. "Certainly the blows could have been struck by a young man in good health?"

A. "Certainly."

The fussy Featherstone, however, had a few instincts of the courtroom counselor. Up he bounced at this moment, as the prosecutor sat down, to put the obvious question. He couldn't have liked the answer.

Q. "Now, Doctor, I put it to you that the person who
struck down this poor lady with such a powerful
weapon, causing her to bleed copiously, must inevitably
have got some of the blood upon his clothing? Enough,
in fact, that he could not have concealed it?"

A. "Not necessarily. Normally there is very little bleeding, or none, from a depressed skull fracture such as we
have here—a small amount from the ear, perhaps. The
relevant damage is not external, you understand. It is
my considered opinion, from evidence at the scene, that
the fracture was caused by the first blow—she fell to the
floor, and was then struck further blows which caused
practically all of the bleeding. The murderer, bending
above her to strike those blows with a weapon as long
as the poker, is not likely to have gotten blood on his
clothes, as no artery was severed."

Regina Moore was called briefly to describe the finding of
the body. The trial was now in its fifth day; the first had gone
to getting the jury seated—surprising that hadn't taken longer.
But now at last came Mrs. Jean Clark, and even at second
hand, in cold typescript, her testimony came through uncom-
promising, unequivocal.

The prosecutor took her through a little background. Yes,
she had worked for Mrs. Tredgold for nearly twelve years,
knew her well. She was nice to work for, generous and considerate. Yes, she had liked Mrs. Tredgold very much.

Q. "Were you aware, before the day of the crime, that
there had been quarrels between Mrs. Tredgold and the
rest of her family?"

A. "It wasn't any of my business, what went on between
them. I wouldn't hear nothing about that anyway, I was
only there in the afternoons three times a week, and
they didn't come in the afternoon much—she'd be at one
of their houses for dinner, or them at her place."

Q. "So you were surprised when you overheard Mrs.
Tredgold quarreling with her nephew that afternoon?"

A. "Mr. Dick always had a temper on him. They both did. But I was some surprised at that."

Q. "You knew he was coming to the house?"

A. "Yeah, she told me his wife wanted to borrow the punch bowl set, and for me to get out the box."

Q. "What time did Mr. Tredgold arrive?"

A. "About five o'clock or a bit past. I let him in and called upstairs to tell her he was there. Then I went and got the punch bowl and cups out of the dining room and took them into the kitchen and put them in the box. And I took the box back to the front hall ready for him."

Q. "At that time, was Mrs. Tredgold in the living room with her nephew?"

A. "Sure. He was hollering at her what a fool she was for letting somebody con her out of money, and she was giving back as good as she got."

Q. "You could not see either of them because the door was shut?"

A. "That's right. I don't know what good they thought it was, shut the door, when you could hear them all over the house."

Q. "Then you cannot tell the court how Mrs. Tredgold was dressed?"

A. "I can give a pretty good guess. I knew the way she did things. She'd gone up to get ready—she was going out someplace and she said somebody was picking her up a little bit after six—and she went upstairs about four-fifteen. She didn't like to hurry herself, but she always liked to be right on time, going someplace. She had a bath, I heard the water running out, and then she'd have got her underthings on and made up her face, put on perfume and all, and my guess'd be that right about the time Mr. Dick came she was all dressed ready to go."

Q. "But you didn't see her to swear to that? All right. You were ready to leave yourself?"

A. "That's right. I always left at five-thirty. Usually I'd say good night to her but they was going at it so hot in there I didn't, just left. I went out the front door, my car was in front."

Q. "Do you know the exact time?"

A. "It was just five-thirty. There's a clock in the front hall, it always keeps good time, and it said five-thirty. I stopped to get my tank filled at a station on Santa Monica and there's a big clock there, it said five thirty-five then."

Q. "And when you left, Mrs. Tredgold was in the living room, having a heated argument with her nephew—or rather, he with her?"

A. "Sure, I just said so."

There wasn't much any lawyer could do with a witness like that: obstinate, pigheaded, absolutely sure. In Featherstone's place, Jesse thought he might not have tried. In a way, Featherstone had just made it worse. The more he had coaxed her, could she be so sure of the exact time, wasn't it possible that aunt and nephew had simply been having an absorbing conversation on a subject interesting to them both, the more obstinate she got.

Q. "I put it to you, Mrs. Clark, that your interpretation of what you say you overheard was mistaken, that in reality—"

A. "I know what I heard and saw. Just because I go out doing housework for people doesn't say I'm a fool. I've told you what happened, and that's what did happen."

Inexorably the prosecutor moved on to the defendant. After he was settled on the stand (three months of waiting in jail for the trial, six days now of the elaborate courtroom ritual, and the double row of jurors' faces staring at him), he was led gently through the preliminaries.

Q. "—had resented this new interest of your aunt's? That is, you and the rest of the family? You had quarreled repeatedly with her about it?"

A. "I don't know what you mean by 'resented.' We had been amused by it at first, but when we found out she intended to give this woman quite a lot of money, we had tried—my brother and I—to reason with her. We thought—"

Q. "Please speak up, Mr. Tredgold, the court did not hear that remark."

A. "—felt that it was a passing fad with her, she'd never been interested in things like that before, and she'd regret it later. It was a large amount of money."

Q. "And of course it was family money? You resented seeing this large amount of money pass out of the family?"

A. "I don't know what the hell you mean by that. It was her own money, we just thought she was being foolish."

Q. "Please do not use profanity to the court, Mr. Tredgold. At any rate, there had not been a complete estrangement between Mrs. Tredgold and the rest of you? You were nominally on speaking terms?"

A. "Well, for—yes, of course. There was never any question of estrangement. It's ridiculous to—"

Q. "Please just answer my questions, sir. So that your wife felt free to ask Mrs. Tredgold for the loan of this punch bowl, and you to drop by the West Hollywood house to pick it up? Mrs. Clark let you in and proceeded to go to get the punch bowl. Did your aunt come down to you at once?"

A. "Yes, in just a minute."

Q. "How was she dressed?"

A. "She was wearing a cotton housecoat. She said she was going out, she was nearly finished dressing. I asked if she was going to a séance with her new friends. I admit it was the wrong thing to say, I should have known better. I was trying to—"

Q. "Please raise your voice, sir. What did you say?"

A. "—trying to keep it light. But she came back with something that annoyed me, and I said we'd never thought she was a fool but I was starting to change my mind. I would like to say definitely that I was not shouting, nor was she, and that the door of the room was open. It was never shut. You keep talking about arguments, well, there never were any arguments over this damn fool thing, not in the sense you seem to think. We were simply exasperated with her and trying to make her see sense. And to anticipate your next question, what was exasperating was just how she annoyed me that day—she simply would not discuss realities. It was just the same that time. She was very consciously patient and forgiving with me, and kept telling me I would soon see the error of materialistic thinking if I could open my mind to the realities of the astral world. I'm afraid I was rather rude to her. I said I hadn't time to talk nonsense. I wasn't feeling in the mood to be very patient with her, it was a damned hot day and the air conditioning was out in the car. I wanted to get home. I told her to have a good time, and went out to the hall—"

Q. "You told her to have a good time?"

A. "Yes, of course. Haven't you realized, for God's sake, that all this talk about quarrels and arguments is just so much guff? We were a family—families have fights and disagreements, they don't break up. We thought she was being a damn fool, but—"

Q. "We really cannot have disrespect for the court, Mr. Tredgold. Very well, then what did you do?"

A. "Well, I picked up the box in the hall, went out to my car, and drove home. The last I saw of Aunt Lou she was starting upstairs again, and she told me to drive carefully."

And Jesse felt quite cross with Featherstone; he missed every cue. He didn't mention the punch bowl set once, to point out the absurdity of a man who'd presumably just committed an impulsive violent homicide carefully remembering to take that with him as he fled. The best he could think of, apparently, was to address himself to a time-honored formula.

Q. "Mr. Tredgold, did you love your aunt—this cultured, respectable lady who had opened her home to you and your brother when you were orphaned, had given you every care and comfort as though you had been her own children?"

A. "Yes, of course."

Q. "Mr. Tredgold, would you take your solemn oath that you never raised your hand in anger and violence against this woman you loved so tenderly?"

A. "Certainly."

Oh, ow, thought Jesse. After that, of course, the prosecutor simply stood up on cross-examination to ask one question.

Q. "Mr. Tredgold, are you a regular communicant of any religious institution?"

A. "No."

Jesse sat back and shut his eyes. *Man looks on the outward appearance, but the Lord looks on the heart,* he quoted to himself sadly. The rest would be practically anticlimax. And he saw what Wheelock meant; Tredgold hadn't helped his own case one damn bit.

There was the testimony of the neighbor who saw him arrive home, reasonably positive of the time because he'd been listening to the six o'clock news about ten minutes. Testimony of Mrs. Alida Tredgold who swore to the same thing. There were two college friends who testified unhappily that Tredgold had a hot temper.

Mrs. Rena Werner, as the inadvertent witness, had really clinched the case.

Q. "—reside at such an address on Sylvia Drive? From your front yard, you have an unobstructed view of Mrs. Louise Tredgold's home at such an address on the same street?"

A. "Yes."

Q. "On the afternoon of August 16, you were busy at

some garden work in your front yard, from about what
time?"

A. "I went out about four o'clock. We have a gardener
who does the lawn and so on but I enjoy gardening and
I do a lot of it myself. I was weeding the flower beds
along the sidewalk, so I was facing the street. It was
very quiet, no one seemed to be out. Of course it was a
hot day."

Q. "You were keeping track of the time?"

A. "Well, yes. I wanted to go in about six, to start dinner. My husband gets home about six-thirty."

Q. "Will you tell the court what activity you noted on
the street during that time? Oh, perhaps you had also
better make clear just how close the Tredgold house is
to yours."

A. "It's on the corner opposite. Our house is the third
one down from the corner. There wasn't any activity. I
suppose most people were inside in air conditioning. I
saw a car stop in front of Mrs. Tredgold's house—"

Q. "Excuse me, were you acquainted with her?"

A. "No, we just knew her by sight. Before that, there'd
only been one car along the street. It was Mrs. Parr, she
lives two doors down, I knew her car. She parked in her
driveway and went in. This car parked in front of the
corner house about, oh, a few minutes after five. I had
my watch on, yes."

Q. "What kind of car was it?"

A. "It was a bright red Buick. I thought I'd seen it there
before."

Q. "Did you see another car near that house?"

A. "There was an old sedan of some kind parked around
the corner. After a while a woman came out and drove
away in that. I didn't notice her particularly, I just
heard the car start and glanced up."

Q. "You have never employed Mrs. Jean Clark in any ca-
pacity?"

A. "No."

Q. "Please be very careful, Mrs. Werner, of how you answer this question. Can you estimate the length of time between the departure of the old sedan and that of the Buick?"

A. "I couldn't be absolutely sure. It wasn't very long. At least five minutes, I think, maybe more. I didn't see him —anybody—get into the Buick. But it started up—well, with a little noise, and I looked up, and it was just going off, rather fast."

A. "Did you look at your watch?"

Q. "Not right then, no. I looked a few minutes later, because I knew it was after five-thirty, and it was nearly a quarter of six."

Q. "Between the time you saw the Buick drive off and the time you went into the house—when did you go in?"

A. "At six o'clock exactly."

Q. "—What activity was there on the block?"

A. "Well, none. There wasn't anybody on the street at all, or any cars passing. It was very quiet and still, sort of breathless—it was so hot, you know. Excuse me, there was someone, but—"

Q. "Yes?"

A. "Next door, on the front steps, the little Walsh boy was there with another boy I didn't know. They were playing with model airplanes or something, I didn't pay attention. The other boy went off down the street, the other way, just before I went in."

Q. "Thank you very much, Mrs. Werner."

There wasn't much more. Featherstone called Walt Tredgold, for no apparent reason, to say that he'd seen his brother in the company offices on Olympic Boulevard in Santa Monica that afternoon at about four-thirty, and had known his brother was to see their aunt. That he himself had left the office at five-thirty, driven home, and had dinner with his wife and two children. That he was notified of the homicide at approximately eight-forty by a sheriff's deputy. Rebecca Tredgold had testified that she was familiar with the habits of her husband's aunt, and would not say that she was particularly careful about being dressed early for any engagement.

The closing arguments were more redundancy and ritual. The judge, in instructing the jury, was perhaps less than impartial against the defendant.

Jesse was surprised the jury had been out as long as an hour.

What it came down to was which one you believed, Clark or Tredgold. But either way, the big stumbling block was Rena Werner.

Clark—deliberately malicious? (The door open?) But why? Dick Tredgold had impressed the jury unfavorably. But Rena Werner describing that hot, still, empty August street— Just what other answer could there be? The jury had bought the simple answer.

FOUR

End of case. Rather a short trial, as trials went. The sentencing, the appeal, the denial of appeal, would have occupied another couple or three months.

Jesse realized that he was starving. It was nearly one o'clock. He handed over the box of microfilm, the projector, to the clerk at the desk and walked half a block from the courthouse to a hamburger stand where he consumed a cheeseburger absently. He thought about Jean Clark; but the mysterious boy friend intrigued him a good deal.

He went back to the public lot for the Mercedes and drove down to Santa Monica. There wasn't any answer to the doorbell at the Tredgold house, but as he got back into the car a Pontiac turned into the drive with Becky Tredgold alone in it. Jesse got out again.

She looked at him in surprise and a little vexation. "I've got all this marketing to put away—"

"No hurry," said Jesse. She let him in the back door, to a bare and neat kitchen; he sat in the comfortable living room while she rattled around out there opening and shutting the freezer door, cupboards. After a while she came to join him, sat down on the couch and lit a cigarette.

"I'm sorry, I was just rather surprised to see you."

"Sorry to bother you. I just wanted to ask—"

"I don't see what good it is, that's all—you raking it up all over again! It's just brought it all back."

"Well, a couple of things have shown— I've got a couple of ideas," said Jesse vaguely. "What I wanted to ask you—I don't suppose the three girl friends were all she had? Did she belong to any clubs? Do you know who her other friends were?"

Becky said impatiently, "Well, of course she had lots of friends. Most of them, oh, casual, but people she knew, yes. A good many women she knew had husbands attached—it's sometimes awkward for a single woman, people tend to invite by couples—but she belonged to the West Ebell Club, and I know there was a bridge club she went to every week. Well, I really couldn't tell you any names—just first ones she'd mention casually, Jane, Alice, Polly—you understand, Mr. Falkenstein, we all had our own lives to lead, she was busy and active—I knew generally what she was doing, maybe twice a month she'd be here to dinner, or ask us over. But—"

"I suppose," said Jesse, "it's silly to ask about her address book."

"Good heavens," said Becky in sole comment. "Everything like that got thrown out when we were clearing up the house, getting it ready to sell. She didn't write many letters, I know that. The only regular correspondent she had was a woman she'd known a long time here, who remarried and moved to Chicago, and I'm blessed if I can remember—Moira Cheney, that was it. My God, how this has brought it all back—" She inhaled deeply, leaning back on the couch. "I remember writing the woman a note telling her what had happened—everybody else she knew would be seeing the papers. A nice social problem, how to write a stranger and say, so sorry to tell you, but your old friend's just been murdered."

The Ebell Club, my God, thought Jesse. How many members? "The members of the bridge club?"

"That was a regular weekly thing, I know. Polly—Polly—Polly Demarest. I think. I don't suppose that helps you, I don't know her husband's name. But none of those women would know anything, I can't see—"

"Have you got any pictures of her?" asked Jesse suddenly. It had just occurred to him that he didn't know what Louise Tredgold had looked like.

"Oh, for heaven's sake—" She bit her lip, thinking. "We've never gone in much—but maybe in that old album—" She went away, was gone for ten minutes, came back with a big Kodak album. "I think these are mostly from that year or just before. Alida'd got Dick interested in photography, he had a new camera." She leafed over pages, handed him the album open. "There. That's Aunt Lou and Walt together by the pool."

A younger Walt Tredgold, in bright summer sun, wearing Bermuda shorts, laughing into the camera. The woman beside him—she didn't look fifty-six, a pretty little woman, with a pansy-kitten face, frosted blond hair in a feathery cut, a pert nose. He handed the album back with a nod.

"Was she friendly with any of the neighbors, do you know?"

"The woman next door, yes. She was an invalid of some kind, arthritis I think, and Aunt Lou felt sorry for her. She used to go in to see her once a week or so, take her candy or magazines. Shellabarger, her name was—Charlene Shellabarger."

"Where," asked Jesse, "did she acquire the Clark woman, do you know?"

"I haven't the slightest idea. She was already working there when Walt and I were married, that's eighteen years ago. It could have been a newspaper ad, or somebody recommending her, anything." She put out the cigarette, stood up. "Raking it all over—no point, and I've got that roast to put in—"

"Yes, sorry to take up your time," said Jesse. "Thanks very much."

When Louise hadn't told Celia Adams anything definite—but you never knew what a woman might tell whom. And he wondered if the Clark woman was still working anywhere in that neighborhood.

West Hollywood was a cut above Hollywood, on the verge of Beverly Hills and Trousdale Estates. There were elegant apartments, new condominiums, there was business; but the older residential streets of single houses were less showy. He looked at Sylvia Drive with interest. It was a short street, only three blocks long, tucked away behind blocks of similar streets away from any main drag. This block was the shortest. He could imagine it that hot August day, nothing stirring: the big gracious older houses dozing in the shimmering heat. They were quietly elegant houses, looking to be conscious of being in an excellent residential area, behind manicured green lawns. A lawn mower was running somewhere, a few cars parked along the street. He idled up the block, looking for addresses.

The lawn mower was at work on the side lawn of the corner house. Louise Tredgold's house. It was a two-story English-style house, beige stucco with red brick trim, chimney, and iron-railed front porch: a very handsome house. The gardener propelling the lawn mower was a stolid-looking Mexican. The garage was shut, and no car stood in the drive.

Jesse left the Mercedes in front of it and went up the brick walk of the house next door, a pseudo-Tudor place with dark beams nailed on white stucco. The woman who opened the door was pleasant-faced, plumply middle-aged.

"Shellabarger?" she said blankly, and then, "Oh, of course that's who we bought the house from two years ago. I'm afraid I couldn't tell you anything about her, where she is now. All I know is, the real estate woman said she was left alone when her husband died, and she was an invalid, couldn't live alone, so the house was for sale and I believe she'd moved into a rest home. The post office might still have a forwarding address."

Unlikely, thought Jesse. He thanked her, started back to the Mercedes. The house on the corner looked singularly empty.

But as he opened the driver's door, a bright blue Renault sports model came sailing around the corner and turned into the driveway there. Out of it got a young fellow in neat casual sports clothes, and went up to the gardener with the lawn mower. Jesse shut the car door and sauntered up the front walk.

As he approached them, the young fellow looked round in casual enquiry. "Excuse me, not selling anything," said Jesse, "but I wonder if you could tell me if there's anyone living around here since eight or nine years back."

"Well, sure, we were. And a few other—" He took the card Jesse offered. He was nineteen or twenty, good-looking without being handsome, with pleasantly rugged features, curly dark hair not too long, steady blue eyes. Jesse cocked his head at him, bits of the transcript returning to his mind.

"Would you be Mr. Walsh by any chance?" The Walsh boy. The people across the street who bought the house.

"That's me—Bob Walsh. What's a lawyer want here?" He wasn't belligerent, just interested.

"I'd like to talk with anyone who was living around here at the time Mrs. Louise Tredgold was murdered. You remember that?"

"My Lord, yes," said Bob Walsh. "We bought the house— this was her house, where it happened." The gardener, trudging back and forth behind the lawn mower, came up to them, turned, and trudged away again. "What's it all about?"

"Well, I'm looking into the case again. Kind of semiofficially, you could say."

Bob Walsh looked astonished and curious. "You aren't telling me some new evidence has shown up on that—after all this time? A lawyer—looking into it all over—"

"This and that's certainly shown up," said Jesse truthfully.

"Well, I will be damned!" said young Walsh frankly. "Mom's going to be mad as blazes she missed this, all I can say. Look, would you like to come in—see the house?"

"Thanks, I would."

Bob got out a key ring, started up the brick walk. "I can't get over it. Just luck you caught me—I cut a study period, had to get back to pay Manuel, it's his payday. Well, of course, he was here too, he worked for Mrs. Tredgold then—does most places on this block. I can't get over it. New evidence. Mom's going to be furious she wasn't here." He unlocked the heavy oak-grained front door. "She always said that fellow they got for it didn't do it."

The entrance hall was generous, nearly square; an open door to the left led down two steps to a wide living room, a door to the right to a formal dining room, and at the rear of the hall a curving staircase rose. Almost, for a flash, Jesse saw the trim little ghost of Louise Tredgold flitting up it.

"Is that a fact?" he said. "Why did she think that?"

Bob Walsh shut the front door behind them. He looked now, a little uncertain. "Well—" he said. "Would you like to sit down, Mr. Falkenstein? It's a shame they're not here—Mom and Dad. They're on a three-month cruise in the Orient, Mom finally persuaded him to take some time off. I'm sort of holding down the old home place, alone. Oh, Mrs. Bloom comes in to fix dinner"—he laughed—"Mom said I'd be living on hamburgers otherwise. I'm in my first year at U.S.C.—law."

"Not the easiest way to make a living," said Jesse, sitting down at one end of the couch. The boy couldn't be much over nineteen, but he was mature for that age, the blue eyes aware and intelligent.

"Maybe you know, we lived right across the street when it happened, the murder. My mother always liked this house, and of course my two sisters were still at home then—they're both married now. When it was up for sale, we bought it."

"Not worried about ghosts?"

Bob laughed. "If there had been one, Mom would have been thrilled. She's very much into the psychic bit, I mean the real serious stuff, not just ghost stories and Ouija boards. The real research. We've got quite a library of stuff on all that. I'm interested too. I don't know if you—know anything about all that, or what you think about it—"

"Done a good deal of reading. Why?"

"Oh," said Bob. "Have you? I suppose you couldn't tell me about what the new evidence is."

Jesse grinned at him; he liked this young fellow, an engaging mixture of mature youth and still slightly ingenuous adolescence. "You were mentioned in the trial, you know. I've just been over the transcript."

"I was? How'd I get into it?"

"Mrs. Werner—she still live across the street?"

"No, they retired to Sun City last year."

"That figures," said Jesse. "Evidently she doesn't mind the heat. Her out gardening on a day like that, middle of August. She'd like the desert. She was the one who testified that nobody came down the street after Dick Tredgold left. You know any of the details of the case?"

"Oh, sure—we've talked about it a lot. Especially back then. Of course there was a lot in the papers, and Mom cut most of it out to keep. She had a theory, see. After we moved in here—well, she got all those clippings to read over. She always said that fellow wasn't guilty."

"She have any concrete reason?"

Bob hesitated and then said, "I don't know what you'd think about it, sir. But you said you've read some— You see, we bought some of the furniture in the house. The pieces Mom liked. The dining room set, and that coffee table, and one of the bedroom sets, and the roll-top desk in the den. And the clock in the front hall. It's an antique, the clock. And for nearly two years after we moved in, that clock stopped at the same time every day."

Jesse sat up. "Oh, really."

"That's right. It's an eight-day windup clock. Made in Germany about a hundred years ago. Mom knows about antiques. When it's running, it always keeps good time, right to the minute. But that couple of years, every day it stopped at the same time. Five forty-seven."

"Now I will be damned," said Jesse softly.

"It got so we expected it. Somebody would start it going again, and it ran just fine—till the next day. Mom thinks it means that's the time she was murdered."

And of course it wasn't evidence that could be offered in court. But in the long annals of the queer things that went on stubbornly happening, despite rational science's inability to explain them—even when rational science deigned to look at them—as well as in the respected annals of all the experiments in psychokinesis—the clocks were the most persistent. Usually stopped clocks; sometimes inexplicably starting clocks; even clocks whose dials got twisted. But in how many thousands of documented cases, the clock stopping on the death of an owner. Never mind the mechanism, or the reason.

"How did I come into the trial?"

"Hm?" If she had been killed at five forty-seven, of course it was impossible for Dick Tredgold to have done it. And it was a plausible time. Him leaving at five thirty-five; her going back upstairs to take off the housecoat, put on her dress—five minutes?—and then what?—hearing a noise downstairs, coming down— "What? Oh, Mrs. Werner said you were on the front steps next door, with another boy."

"Was I? I suppose that'd have been Stan Goodrich—we used to be pals then. It's funny how things fade into each other in your memory. And it'd have been an ordinary day—except, I remember the police cars coming when we were having dinner. It's kind of hazy—of course we talked about it a lot, afterward, and that sort of brought it back. I know Stan and I tried to think back, if we'd seen anything suspicious. Kids trying to play detectives." Bob laughed. "We were both eleven, you know kids. I know it was that day something came up and Mom couldn't drive us to the swimming pool, so we were just hanging around all day. Sometime earlier that afternoon, we'd tried to tag after Mike Palfrey and Dave Warren—we were always doing that, and they always chased us off, they were thirteen, fourteen and called us little kids. It was the end of summer vacation, when there wasn't much to do and we were really bored. But that's funny, my getting mentioned at the trial." He was watching Jesse. "You really think that clock means something, don't you?"

"It's nothing I'd lay in front of a judge. But I do indeed. Too many cases in the records of the same thing happening—it means something."

"I can't get over this new evidence bit. I don't suppose, even if it's something definite, you could let it out before the legal part—but we'd sure be interested to know. Say, Mr. Falkenstein, would you like to look over the house? See where it happened, I mean?"

"I would. Thanks," said Jesse. But, following Bob out to the front hall, he paused to look at the clock. It was a dignified-looking clock, hanging on the wall at right angles to the front door: a pleasantly carved dark oak clock with a pendulum. The pendulum was swinging silently, regularly. "When did it stop doing it?" he asked.

"Dad finally took it to a repair place and they cleaned it, said there wasn't anything wrong with it. Then it only stopped about once a week, and then after a while about once a month, and for three or four years now it's never done it again. Mom kept track of it. She thought there might be some—you know, manifestation—in the house besides. Like Mrs. Tredgold trying to come back, or communicate—but there never was." Bob sounded a little naïvely regretful on that.

———————

Jesse looked in the door of his office at five-thirty and found the Gordons just ready to leave. "Some little jobs for you in the morning, girls."

"You've had eleven clients calling for appointments," said Jean, "and I finally started telling people you're in bed with flu."

"Good as anything." And he didn't think he was going to try to track down the various lady members of the West Ebell Club who might have known Louise eight years ago, but he could make an effort where success was more possible, if remote. "I'd like to find an old lady named Charlene Shellabarger. She probably went to a rest home about two years ago as a permanent patient. I've no idea which one."

Jimmy looked at him, outraged. "Do you have any notion how many rest homes there are in the greater L.A. area? It'd take a month of Sundays—and they wouldn't give out any information about patients, even names."

"Say you're trying to track down the heir to a legacy. They'll part with the name, if you find her. At the moment it's eight-thirty in Chicago, but first thing in the morning one of you can go to the library and locate a private eye there. I want him to find a Moira Cheney, hopefully resident there somewhere."

"Just what are you doing, anyway?" asked Jean.

"I wish I was sure myself."

He told Nell all about it over dinner, and she listened interestedly. "Odds and ends," he said, holding out his cup for a third refill of coffee. "This and that, that didn't show up at the time. That you can think about. But where the hell any of it points— This mysterious boy friend. Damn it, Nell, a woman like that—a lady, a good looker even at her age, all the money— she wouldn't have taken up with just any man. She wasn't man crazy, she'd been a widow for six years without giving any signs of hunting another husband. It'd have to have been somebody presentable, in a fairly good job, her own class—a man she could be reasonably sure wasn't after her money—she wasn't an absolute fool. Why was she so mysterious about it, and why didn't he show up afterward?"

"I might offer a guess on that," said Nell, lighting another cigarette. "She'd met this man, and they liked each other. And you know, Jesse, another thing we can deduce, she didn't meet him in the ordinary way, getting introduced by a mutual friend—or am I woolgathering? I think if she had, the minute the Adams woman heard that little confidence, she and the other woman would have been speculating as to who, this unattached man or that, who Louise knew. And they hadn't an idea. So possibly she'd met him just casually—got talking at the market or somewhere—and she was feeling a little self-conscious about that. But the rest of it—say, they'd taken to each other, probably been out together—nobody need have known, the family weren't keeping tabs on her. There are nuances in these things, after all. It could be that she was almost sure he was going to ask her to marry him, but he hadn't yet. So she just hinted, because it wasn't sure yet."

"But why didn't he show up later? If he was that serious about her, thought that much of her, wouldn't he have gone to the funeral? Introduced himself to the family? Or, of course—" Jesse stopped and drank coffee.

"Yes," said Nell dryly, "would you? She hadn't introduced

him to the family, all he knew was what she'd told him about them. And first she's murdered, and then—before the funeral—her nephew's arrested for the murder. Don't you think he'd just have kept quiet about the whole episode?"

"That's supposing nobody at all knew they knew each other."

"Which is possible."

"All up in the air. But what isn't," said Jesse, "is the behavior of that Clark woman. The jury believed her over Tredgold, but if we take it that he was telling gospel truth, she was telling a pack of lies. About the door, about the dress, about the hot argument."

"Yes. Why didn't Wheelock go after her, after she told lies at the trial? Or the defense attorney? After all, there was an appeal pending—"

"Wheelock wasn't on the case any more, he'd finished any investigation before the trial. He didn't find out anything definite about the woman then. The defense attorney—he probably talked to her, but I don't think he'd get far with that one. Damn it, why should she deliberately tell those lies, clinching the whole case against Tredgold?"

Nell shook her head. "It's not as if she'd been an old family retainer, with any emotional interest in the Tredgolds. Just the paid domestic help. I can't see what ax she might have had to grind. Unless—I suppose it could be that she was very fond of Louise, convinced Dick was guilty, and wanted to be sure he didn't get off."

"I don't read her that way, but I can't make head or tail of that testimony anyway. Bob Walsh didn't know whether she's still working for anybody around there. If I can locate her to talk to, something may emerge. How the hell did I get involved in this shapeless damned thing, anyway?"

Nell laughed. "You know what I was thinking when you were telling me about it? Old Edgar would have been fascinated—just the kind of case he loved to worry at."

"Well, I wish he'd tap one of William's tame psychics on the shoulder and pass me a hint," said Jesse.

Clock had come home tired and annoyed at the endless thankless job, and was welcomed affectionately by the black Peke Sally and Fran. Thoughtfully, Fran fed him steak, french fries, asparagus, hot rolls, and apple pie to follow, and Clock announced that he felt better. He retreated amiably into the living room while she dealt with the dishes and went on to do some personal laundry.

When she came into the living room three quarters of an hour later she found him ensconced, shoeless and tieless, in the big armchair with his feet on the ottoman and Sally snuggled in the crook of one arm sound asleep. He was absorbed in *Crime and the Psychic World.*

He looked up at her vaguely. "Say, this is damned interesting. It all seems to be documented, straight facts. I hadn't realized how some other police forces really take this seriously, even call in mediums sometimes."

"Your stuffy old L.A.P.D. a little behind the times," said Fran.

"Well, I wouldn't say—we're using hypnosis a good deal now, but that's not exactly the same thing." Clock went back to his book, and Sally started to snore.

On Tuesday morning Jesse started out to locate Jean Clark. There was a discouragingly long list of Jean Clarks, J. Clarks, and assorted Clarkes, in all six phone books; she might be there, but it would take days to work through the list, and he'd rather not give her warning that somebody was looking for her, with questions out of the past. If he could drop on her via a short cut—

He started on Sylvia Drive, methodically plodding door to door. Today the Mexican gardener was at a house three doors down from the Walshes'. He didn't find anyone who recognized Clark's name until he got to the end of the block and Mrs. Camden.

"Yes, she worked for me at one time, but she doesn't now and I don't know where she lives, all I ever had was a phone number."

"Would you still have it?"

"Oh no, she hasn't worked for me for two years. Could I ask why—"

"Friend of ours up the block mentioned to my wife that Mrs. Shellabarger used to have a good cleaning woman—very difficult to find now, you know."

She regarded him curiously. Evidently she didn't connect Clark with an old murder case; she might be new in the neighborhood. "Oh, I see. Well, I don't know that I'd give Mrs. Clark a recommendation. She's a funny sort of woman—a good enough worker, but—" She compressed her lips. "Well, I'm sorry if I'm wronging her, but the reason I let her go, I'm almost sure she took some money from my bag the last time she was here. It wasn't the amount—five dollars—but you can see—"

He didn't get a smell of her anywhere else along the block. And you never knew: eight years was a while for a woman like that to stay in one rented place, maybe, but she could still be there. He found the address on Berendo in Hollywood: it was a little frame house at the rear of the lot behind a larger house in front. She wasn't there. A thin blonde who didn't look fifteen but who was indifferently nursing a baby told him she'd never heard of Mrs. Clark, and that the landlady lived in the front house.

He tried there. A motherly looking white-haired woman said at once, "Jean Clark? Why, yes, she lived here, rented the rear house, up to about three years ago. She had one girl still with her, t'other one got married. We had to put the rent up, everything getting so high, my husband retired and all, and she couldn't make it. But I believe I could tell you where she moved to, not that we ever heard from her but I had the address on account of mail, and Fred says I never throw anything away—just a minute, I'll see." She came back in ten minutes with a scrap of paper, a scribbled address on it. "Oh, don't bother copying it, I got no use for it."

It was Santa Ynez Street; he had to consult the County Guide to find it—downtown, near Echo Park.

By this time it was noon, and on a weekday the traffic was thick down there. It was a narrow old street of duplexes and four-family apartments. The address he wanted was one of those, the rear upper left of a square ugly box of a building with packed dirt in a strip of front yard and broken cement steps to four narrow doors. The name slot on the mailbox said *Raines,* but he pushed the bell anyway. Nobody answered.

The next mailbox-slot said *Clancy;* he pushed that bell and a fat woman in a flowered muu-muu opened the door. "Clark?" she said to his question. "Yeah, I knew her. She only lived here about six, eight months. Good riddance. People here might be poor, but like to think they're honest. Godawful commotion, middle o' one night, it's cops after them—her and her daughter, they were selling dope or something. Anyway, the landlord told her to get out, and I never laid eyes on her since."

It was threatening to rain again.

What was that wild little scenario he had dreamed up off the top of his mind, about Clark? The pro burglar boy friend? They had said she had no apparent reason to come out with those lies at the trial, to clinch the case against Dick Tredgold; but wouldn't she have had a dandy reason if she knew who the real X was and could be connected to him? Suddenly Jesse thought, that service station stop—maybe she had needed gas, but maybe she'd stopped there five minutes after leaving Louise Tredgold's house to provide herself with a nice alibi?

Did she have, he wondered also suddenly, or had she ever had, a key to the house? Louise Tredgold, gadding around to the Ebell Club, to her bridge games, might not have been at home to let the cleaning woman in every Monday, Wednesday, and Friday.

And the rear screen door hadn't been hooked.

He could bear to know about the key.

He got back on Sunset, heading for Hollywood again, and

stopped at the first pay phone. Becky Tredgold sounded annoyed when she recognized his voice, but a little interest quickened in hers at his question.

"That woman. No, she didn't have a key to the house. She was supposed to come at eleven-thirty or noon, Aunt Lou would be there practically always—and if she was going out, all Mrs. Clark had to do was slam the door to lock it. I do know, though, that when Aunt Lou went to Hawaii—that was about a year before—she did give her a key. She—Aunt Lou—was gone for two weeks, and she let Mrs. Clark have a key so she could go in and dust, take the mail in. But, Mr. Falkenstein—"

"Mmh?"

"I didn't like the woman, I thought she was sly and sneaking, but all that time she worked there, Aunt Lou never had reason to suspect her of being dishonest. Or she wouldn't have kept her, of course. It was just my idea that she'd taken that ruby brooch, and I could be wrong."

"Yes. Was there a safe in the house? Her jewelry kept in it?"

"No, she never would. There was a safe, yes, and she kept things like important papers in it, the pink slip to the car and so on, but she always said it was a nuisance, getting out jewelry when she wanted to wear it. She just kept it in her room."

"Yes, thanks." Jesse hung up absently on her beginning question.

She could have had the key copied for sixty cents. And holding it a year before using it? Well, there would have been some rudimentary planning. There had been a good haul of jewelry in that house, and it had been loose, in boxes, just put away in drawers. Loot for the taking. But of course she'd have had better sense than to walk in and take it—she'd have been the first one the cops looked at. Maybe (considering the cops coming in the night) the pro burglar boy friend wasn't such a far-out idea at that. With that key, he could have slid in the back door, no trouble at all, say in the middle of some quiet afternoon—

Ideas followed each other rapidly through Jesse's mind.

Bridge clubs usually had a definite day to meet, and Clark would know when Louise would be out. On a Tuesday, Thursday, Saturday, or Sunday afternoon: Clark ostentatiously not there. Not Thursday, the gardener would be there then. The rear of that house—he had seen it yesterday, and it was an ideal setup. The back yard was walled to five feet, with oleander shrubs higher than the wall, and the house next door was one-storied, no windows overlooked that yard. The house on the other side, facing the side street, had an enormous old avocado tree in its side yard.

How would she make sure the rear screen door wasn't hooked? But—deduce it—the garage was not attached to the house, at the rear of the long drive; and nobody would habitually walk around to the front door, coming home. Ten to one Louise normally came and went by the back door, with that secure dead-bolt lock. The screen wouldn't be hooked.

He would slide in easy and quiet, knowing he was safe. There had probably been silver—flatware, coffee service, whatever. And on the way out, leave the obvious pry marks on a rear window, cut a screen, lift out a pane of glass with the little cutter— Daring daylight burglary. No muss, no fuss, and nothing remotely to do with the respectable cleaning woman.

Suppose the pro burglar boy friend had been in jail, and the job had to be put off till he was out?

But suppose all that was so, what possible connection could it have with the murder?

The woman had deliberately lied on the stand. If you accepted that Dick Tredgold was telling the truth.

As far as Jesse was concerned, that clock vindicated Dick Tredgold quite nicely.

Suddenly Jesse straightened from leaning on the glass wall of the phone booth and quoted the Apocrypha to himself aloud. "'*No wrath above that of a woman.*' By God, I do wonder!" If the next day had been the day they planned to pull the job—and the murder intervened—she might not have known one damned thing about that, but believing he had done it, wouldn't she have been feeling vindictive! Any further chance at all at that loot would be down the drain forever, because the family would be taking it all away—

And for whatever reason, even eight years later, if her testimony was proven false— God, what a legal mess that would be, but—

He came out of the phone booth, loped back to the Mercedes, and drove back to the middle of Hollywood and the handsome new precinct building.

Here he met with temporary delay. Both Clock and Petrovsky were out somewhere. The desk sergeant, recognizing him as a friend of Clock's, said, "Another arson. We've had five in the last four days, you know? Some nut, and a bastard of a thing to work."

Jesse said he could believe it. He didn't know any of the other detectives here well enough to ask a favor.

At loose ends, anxious to follow up on this idea, he wandered back to the car. A nice lot of loot for the taking, all right, if all that was so. He lit a cigarette, thinking it through again. And then another thought hit him and he grinned to himself. Somebody else had missed out on some nice loot when Louise was killed.

Well, kill a little time. He started the engine. He remembered the address Miss Duffy had located.

It was on Melrose just into West Hollywood and a nice, piece of property. Remembering what Celia Adams had said, he wondered who had picked up the tab. It might have started life as a small furniture showroom, something like that; it stood separate with a little parking lot between it and a big pharmacy. It was a white stucco building with a red tile roof and iron grilles on the front windows.

The parking lot was full. He found a slot half a block up and walked back.

There were neat black metal letters set above the grilled double doors: *Spiritual Brotherhood Temple*. Some kind of thick drapes were drawn inside over the door and two rectangular windows on either side. There was a printed card— professionally printed—inside the right-hand front door. *Reli-*

gious services Sunday 11 A.M. *Public demonstration of clair-voyance Tuesday, Thursday* 8 P.M. *Private sittings by appointment,* and a phone number.

Wheelock thought that this pair had just landed here, back then. To set up some kind of operation aimed at the aimless moneyed society women? By what he said, they hadn't had this kind of setup then. The paragraph in a society column in the *Star*—bought and paid for? Jesse wondered. The *Star* was an old established paper, independent; would its columnists do that sort of thing?

At any rate, the woman had evidently caught some fish with whatever bait. They might be misjudging her, at that. There were always enough honest-to-middling females around with a little rudimentary ESP and large ambitions. But you seldom found them in surroundings like this.

Or described as fashionable psychics.

It was getting on to four o'clock and had started to rain again. Jesse started back to the Mercedes, passed a phone booth, and called into his office to see if the girls had found Mrs. Shellabarger.

"Well, thank goodness!" said Jean. "Had you forgotten you've got an appointment at four o'clock?—it was made last week, Mr. Dupar, about a divorce suit. And Mr. Wallingford's coming in in the morning to sign his will."

"I'm coming, I'm coming," said Jesse. He was fifteen minutes late for the appointment, and Mr. Dupar—a new client—was annoyed. It looked like a fairly simple divorce action; the wife was a lush.

Dupar left at five-fifteen, and Jesse asked the twins how they'd been doing on Shellabarger and the private eye.

Jean just looked at him. "The things men can think of for secretaries to do. I have phoned forty-two rest homes and I'm not half through the list. The private detective agency in Chicago wants a retainer of three hundred. Shall I send it?"

"Ouch," said Jesse. "Well, I guess so."

He ought to go home. The rain made a quick rattle on the

tall windows, and the place felt empty after the girls had gone. He lit another cigarette, picked up the phone, and dialed.

On numerous occasions the conscientious Miss Duffy would be there up until six or later. This time DeWitt answered.

"How'd you like to attend a session with a probably fraudulent medium tonight?"

"I wouldn't."

"Come on, William. I want your opinion. You'd spot any tricks where I might not."

"They don't use many tricks these days," said DeWitt tiredly. "Era of materializations and ectoplasm behind us. Human nature's much more helpful."

"I'll pick you up at seven-thirty."

"Oh, hell," said DeWitt.

FIVE

As Jesse and DeWitt came up to the grilled double doors of the neat stucco building a little group of women arrived from the opposite direction. The two men stood back to let them in, DeWitt holding the door politely. There were soft lights inside now. Beyond the doors was a short entry hall with a small table on the left wall beside an open door. To the immediate right was another door discreetly labeled *Rest Rooms*.

The women, as if automatically, filed into the little room to the left, shedding coats and handbags. A man came up from the large room beyond, a big untidily dressed man, middle-aged, with a friendly booming voice. There were also a dozen people in the big room.

"Ah, I thought I heard other arrivals. Mrs. Dunlap, nice to see you here again. And some newcomers—Mrs. Hancock, I see you've brought a friend, how pleasant, I do hope you won't be disappointed in the meeting." His glance raked DeWitt and Jesse casually.

"Just happened to notice the sign," murmured Jesse. "Sounded interesting—thought, drop in and see—" He let it tail off vaguely.

"Everyone's welcome, sir, very glad to have you with us." There was a box on the table labeled in stenciled gold letters *Offerings*. The women unobtrusively approached one by one to slide bills into the slot on its top; five dollars seemed to be the going price. Jesse and DeWitt each followed suit; the woman just ahead of them, a thin spinsterish-looking woman with short pepper-and-salt hair, turned to flash a timid smile at them.

"She's a very good medium, you'll find it interesting."

"I'm Rodney Steele, gentlemen—you're very welcome. May I ask if you are familiar with clairvoyant demonstrations?"

"No, first time either of us—er— Just thought it might be interesting, you know," mumbled Jesse, looking embarrassed.

"Then perhaps I'd better caution you not to move about or approach the medium while she is in trance, it could be very harmful to her. I hope you'll find something of worthwhile interest to you." He gave them a smile nicely adjusted between friendliness and gravity. "My wife acts as our medium, and ordinarily her clairvoyance is reliable, but the power is quite unpredictable. If you'd like to find seats—"

The large room was perhaps fifty feet square, with plain monk's cloth drapes along two walls. There was a low platform at the far end, rows of plain folding chairs; a door beyond the platform led to some rear premises. Instead of overhead lights there were wall sconces along each side of the room, not high-wattage bulbs but creating a pleasant, dim, intimate effect. By the time Jesse and DeWitt found seats, there might have been thirty people in the place. Below the platform there waited a single large upholstered armchair.

Steele fussed about at something to one side of the platform and addressed them chattily. "I'll just see if my wife is arriving —she always rests until the last minute before a demonstration, as most of you know." He bustled up the room, and the front doors closed behind him. From the stereo he'd turned on, very low background music rose, a choir singing hymns.

One of the two women sitting just ahead of Jesse and De-Witt was the one addressed as Mrs. Hancock, who had brought a newcomer. She was saying now to her seat mate, "My dear, I'm sure you'll find it impressive. She's very good. She has an Egyptian guide, you know, his name is Akh-nur-Ra."

"It's just that I've never been to a clairvoyant before—you do wonder if there's anything in it, but when you're sure she's perfectly genuine and honest—"

"Oh, absolutely, Grace! She's brought me such true messages from Billy, and Nita, and so many others—things she couldn't possibly have known."

"If I could just hear something from Mama. Going so suddenly like that— I'm wearing her pearls tonight, I thought it might help the vibrations. The association with her name, you know."

"I'm sure that's a good idea, dear." They were both women in the fifties, one plump, one thin, smartly dressed. Of the rest of the crowd, there was only one man besides Jesse and De-Witt, a sparrowlike little man with a long nose, who sat several chairs away from anyone else. All of the women were well dressed and they looked fairly prosperous. Little groups of them whispered together, and the choir was muted in the background.

Five minutes later Rodney Steele bustled back in. "A trifle late, but here we are at last. My dear—" He stepped back, and Sabrina Steele came past him, up the center aisle, to seat herself in the armchair.

She was rather jolly-looking, a puff-breasted robin of a woman, with short black hair and red cheeks. She might be forty-five. She had on a plain black dress, no jewelry. When she spoke, her voice was low and pleasant, with no particular accent.

"If you'll all just make a silent prayer with me, that the forces around us are good ones, and the channel open—we'll just wait for the guides, and hope something will come."

Gradually the choir dimmed and there was absolute silence. Inevitably, a little shuffling noise: a suppressed cough; a sigh. The medium was now lolling sideways in the chair. She raised herself slightly, and her voice was deeper, with a curious stilted accent.

"Very well, I am here. Akh-nur-Ra is here to help. There are many upon the other side would speak to those still on your side, but it is not always easy that even the higher guides should help them. There are many dark thoughts, dark spirits over the earth of your time. Those whose hearts truly belong to God must be strong for the truth and light—"

There was a good deal more of that, somewhat repetitious, for another three or four minutes, and then the medium fell silent.

"She's in trance now, you know," whispered Mrs. Hancock to her neighbor.

Suddenly the medium sat up again and announced, "There is a spirit here. A W— W— Or is it G— I don't get it clearly— G—or C—the spirit is asking for Ethel. This seems to be a very light, bright spirit—for Ethel—"

"I can't think who it could be," said the spinsterish woman in a small voice. "W— Why, goodness, I wonder if it's Winnie? I hadn't thought of Winnie in years, I didn't know she was on the other side. I lost track of her after high school—"

"The spirit sends kind thoughts to you, to Ethel. You were not close in this life but she has much affection for you. She is smiling, she says there is someone there you both knew, when you were together before, in this life—a B— Betty, Beatrice, B, B, B—"

"Bernice Rinehard, she and Winnie were always together— how funny."

"There are so many spirits wishing to speak. Ah, an old friend, it is William to say good evening to his little sweetheart."

"Oh, Bill," said Mrs. Hancock *sotto voce*. "He's always so faithful about coming, if just for a minute."

"Just for a little moment, because there are so many. Here is one so anxious to speak, one who has not communicated before, I am shown the letter A— Oh, it is a child, there are fair curls and blue eyes—"

A woman behind Jesse uttered a little choking cry. "My little Alice?" she whispered. "I know she'd try to come—"

"Alice comes to tell her mama she is well and happy and only waiting to meet her again. What a pretty child she is! Ah, and here is now another who has not spoken through this in-

strument before. This spirit has not been long on the other side
—it is difficult for her—there are others trying to help. She is
saying—I cannot understand her—ah, yes, no chance to say
good-by, she says. What is it she is saying, a state of grace?—
no, no, it is a name—Grace—Grace—to say good-by, but not forever. I do not understand this, but she keeps gesturing at her
throat, and she says, my name is there."

The woman beside Mrs. Hancock started forward with a
strangled cry. "Mother!" She turned, with the tears starting
down her cheeks. "I didn't believe it was possible—"

"She wants you to know, you are not to grieve for her—all is
well and happy and you will meet again. She is pleased that
you should wear that which represents her name—what can
that be?—ah, pearls, pearls. She is fading now. I am shown the
letter F—ah, it is another old friend, Frances, to speak to
Laura." A stir in the front row. "She is so pleased that Laura's
health is better, and it will be better still if only positive
thoughts are held."

DeWitt sighed and slid down a little in the uncomfortable
slatted chair. Unfortunately, the formula for this kind of entertainment did not allow for an intermission, and it was a good
forty minutes later when the medium interrupted a communication from Louis to his dear friend Barbara to announce,
"This again is Akh-nur-Ra. It is enough, the medium has come
to the end of her current supply of power for this work. She
must rest, great care must be taken of this medium for she has
much strength for good, but she must not overtax this source
of power. Rest, rest, rest. May the light be upon all this company, and the spirit of God go with you. I leave you until the
next meeting."

After a moment the medium sat up. A long rustling stir
passed through the little crowd, and murmurs. "Oh, Ruth, I
never thought it was possible, but you heard her, it had to be
Mother, nobody here knows me—" "A wonderful gift I call it,
didn't I tell you—"

Steele was solicitously bending over his wife, who was

shivering. "I always get so cold," she murmured apologetically to those nearest. He helped her into a thick sweater. Mrs. Hancock and her companion started down the aisle with a few others crowding about the medium. DeWitt gave Jesse one look and they drifted up the other way and out into the clear cold January air.

"And just why you had to inflict that on me— What's your interest in that damned woman, anyway?"

Jesse got out his car keys. "Nice little performance, wasn't it? As you said, human nature is so helpful. I take it the place is bugged?"

"Certainly. Educated guess, the listening post somewhere at the back. Medium ostentatiously arriving in front. You noticed there was an outside door to that anteroom. Handbags handily left there, for somebody to have a quick look at billfolds, drivers' licenses, snapshots. Quick, who did you ever know with the initial D?"

"My father. Of course I know he's not dead. But if I thought twice—I was in high school with a girl named Doris."

"No doubt," said DeWitt dryly. They got into the Mercedes. "Why in hell did we waste a perfectly good evening?"

"Wanted to have a look at the woman. It was a fairly slick performance, William. But would it really convince anybody who wasn't eager to be convinced?"

DeWitt stretched long legs out on the floor of the car and brought out cigarettes. "I ought to be feeling damned annoyed that these—these con artists are still around, but human nature— The hell of it is, we never stumble across many of the genuine psychics, to do the honest-to-God research and study. God knows all of us beleaguered would-be researchers, the last hundred years, have made a desperate effort to build it into a respected scientific field. But while there are still the ones like that floating around," and he jerked a disdainful head at the building down the block, "it will always be so easy for those who don't know a damn thing about it to lump them all together. All mediums are fakes."

"That bunch back there doesn't think Sabrina is." Jesse hadn't started the engine. "Grace at least is convinced she had an evidential message."

"Being in an emotional state, the idea of the bug never occurred to her," said DeWitt tiredly.

"What I'm wondering," said Jesse, "is how she gathered in Aunt Lou. Who wasn't interested at first, until she too got some evidential messages. But she wasn't—mmh—predisposed to believe, not at all, and she wasn't a fool. They must have been pretty convincing communications to have brought her to the point of intending to hand Sabrina fifty G's."

DeWitt yelped, "Fifty grand? To that—that vaudeville artist? Who's Aunt Lou? My God, when I think of how I could use fifty grand—a Faraday cage, a—"

"Oh, she's dead," said Jesse soberly, and started the engine. "She's long dead."

He dropped into the office on Wednesday morning for the appointment with Wallingford, saw the will signed and stashed away, a Xerox copy handed over. Jean was still busy on the phone, and gave him one resigned look. There was a wire in from the private eye acknowledging the wired retainer.

In mid-morning Jesse walked into the detective squad room at the Hollywood precinct and found both Clock and Petrovsky in. "Little favor to ask," said Jesse. "I'd like some information out of your records downtown."

Clock listened to him and said sourly, "Little favor. Using R. and I.'s time for a civilian. Yes, we've got the computers now, but you need some bare information to use them. All you've got is an arrest made on you don't know what date, and a street address. You aren't even sure of the surname."

"I suppose the girl could have been married, but you can try Clark first."

"And there'll be more than one of those," said Clock. "I'll phone it in, but they might not turn it up right away. Give you a ring at the office when it comes through." Clock didn't ask why Jesse was asking, what he was on; he was looking harassed.

"Picked up your arsonist yet?"

"No, we have not. Damned nut setting fires in theaters, phone booths, department store rest rooms, and not a smell. Except that they were mens' rest rooms. My God, why anybody ever picks this job—"

"Don't mind him," said Petrovsky. "He's still fussing about that body. I must say I'm curious myself."

"Where the hell did he *go?*" demanded Clock crossly. "Look, Jesse, maybe you'd have a bright idea on it. Here's a poor old fellow—his name is Milton Peters—decided to commit suicide. He's seventy-nine, a widower, only daughter killed in an accident years ago, he's all alone and he hasn't got much money— Social Security, a little pension. He was a clerk in a men's store till he retired. He's got an artificial leg—developed diabetes about twenty years ago and eventually lost the leg on account of it. He's been living in a two-room apartment down on Mariposa. Been there for years, the other tenants knew him. Woman across the hall, a nice woman, used to keep an eye on him because he was old and frail. So she noticed when he didn't come home that day—a week ago yesterday. She got the landlord to break in—afraid maybe he'd died in there. They didn't find him. What they found was a suicide note addressed to her." Clock opened the top drawer of his desk. "This is what he wrote. 'Dear Mrs. Hansen, I don't want to go on, it is so hard when you get old and life is so empty. I know I'll find my dear wife and little girl waiting, and I hope the Lord understands and doesn't hold it against me I took my own way out. I don't want to make trouble or mess for anybody so I am going out to do it. Please take what little I have in thanks for your kindness, and tell the police it doesn't matter about a funeral, just put me away anywhere.'"

"Poor devil," said Jesse.

"Yes, but where the hell did he go? In the middle of town? Nobody knows whether he had a gun—he could have—but where would he go to use it? The Hansen woman said he used to go to cheap movies, that's all she knew. Well, he's not in any movie house—he's nowhere. Traffic has scoured every alley for blocks, but he'd have been found, for God's sake! And he can't have walked far with his game leg. We know he didn't take a cab anywhere."

"If it was the middle of summer," said Petrovsky, "he'd have been found. Just be patient, Andrew, he'll turn up. I had the bright idea of empty houses, but we looked and there aren't any for a square mile around."

"Well, that is a funny little problem," said Jesse. "I'll be interested to know how it comes out. Meanwhile, I'd be obliged if you try to get that record for me."

"I'll see what I can do." Clock put his hand on the phone, but when Jesse went out he was still studying Mr. Peters' dignified little suicide note.

And after that performance last night Jesse was still wondering about Louise Tredgold and Sabrina. Well, it had been a slick little show. Grace at least was convinced she'd had a real communication, and she'd evidently been reluctant to come. But most of the people who turned out for the public mediums weren't in a critical state of mind.

Louise Tredgold probably had been. Very much so. She'd never been interested in the psychic bit—thinking of Bob Walsh, Jesse smiled. Celia Adams had finally persuaded her to attend one of Sabrina's demonstrations. And she'd been convinced of the validity of communication, and gone back. It was on the cards she'd had private sittings—and he wondered what the going rate for those was. She'd been so convinced—this woman who wasn't a fool, who had helped her husband start a large and successful business—that just a few months later she was eager and willing to hand Sabrina a respectable amount of money. Just how had Sabrina managed to be so persuasive, to produce what seemed to be solid evidential messages?

There was information exchanged about clients, among the fraudulent mediums, but that was generally restricted to the frequenters of spiritualists camps, some of the little far-out sects.

Up to a point, he could see Sabrina acquiring some *sub rosa* information about Louise, but not enough to concoct the messages personal and secret enough to be convincing.

Anyway, he was curious about Sabrina.

After rumination he consulted the phone book and found the newsroom and editorial offices of the Hollywood *News*, occupying the whole second floor of a squat office building on Vermont Avenue. The elevator let him off facing the Classified Advertising desk, and a sign just beyond it said *No Admittance Except Authorized Personnel*. Perforce, he tackled one of the clerks at the Classified desk, a mannish-looking middle-aged woman.

"The society column? Eight years ago? You mean the 'Around Our Town' column? Well, Miss King writes it now, Lucille King, but back then—for years, up to let's see it was six, seven years ago she retired, of course Margaret Mason wrote it. She started it, way back."

"She's retired? Would you know where I can find her?"

"What's it about?"

"Nothing very important. Do you know where she's living?"

She lost interest in him. "I expect she's in the phone book."

She was, at an address in Toluca Lake. It was just noon; Jesse stoppped at a coffee shop on Riverside Drive and killed an hour over lunch. It was one-thirty when he found the address. It was a new-looking condominium, six stories high, with professional landscaping and recessed balconies. She lived in a front unit on the fourth floor.

When the door opened to him, he said, "Miss Mason?"

"Mrs. Mason," she corrected him, smiling. She might be sixty-five or more. She was an ample woman rather than fat, billowing in generous curves all firmly girdled under a plain navy dress. Her skin was very fine and babyishly soft, her iron-gray hair beautifully waved. "What can I do for you?"

Jesse gave her a card. "It'd take too long to explain the circumstances," he said, "but I'm interested in a so-called psychic named Sabrina Steele. I think you once mentioned her when you were still writing a newspaper column. Do you remember anything about her?"

The smile vanished from her mouth. "Why are you interested —a lawyer? She suing or being sued?"

"Neither one. She's very much a side issue to something I'm looking into, is all. I'd be interested in anything you can tell me, and it'll be confidential."

"I don't think that matters," she said. "Come in and sit down." It was a crowded living room, full of furniture and house plants. She sat down in one corner of the couch and Jesse sat facing her. She bent to the coffee table, found a cigarette, and lit it before he could reach his lighter. "I've told the story to enough people, you may as well hear it too. It's not so very ego-building, Mr. Falkenstein, to tell a story on yourself. But it made me so damn mad, not only for my own sake, but thinking what I'd done— Well!" She emitted a stream of smoke, and her eyes were curious on him. "I'd give something to know what your interest is. Circumstances—hah. Well, here's the story, for what it's worth to you.

"I wrote that society column for about eighteen years, a dead bore, but just a job, and it paid. My husband and I never had a family, and I always like to keep busy—I've been a newspaperman all my life. The Beverly Hills and Santa Monica papers syndicated that column, so you can see it reached quite a few readers. And maybe it's an affectation, but I've always used my full name—whenever I had a by-line—since I was married. McKechnie—" she smiled. "It's a good old Scots name and it sounds a little better than plain Maggie Mason. And a column like that gets—chatty." She wrinkled her nose. "Sometimes you run out of things to say. Just so many social affairs and dog shows and theater parties and art shows. Every now and then I'd stick in something personal, reminiscences of earlier-day L.A., mentioning that I was a native. You follow me?"

"Proceed," said Jesse.

"Well, that's background. I'm giving you this just the way it happened. We were living in an apartment in Hollywood then —my husband was a teacher—and I used to work at home. I was proofreading some copy that afternoon when the doorbell rang and there was this woman. Ordinary-looking sort of woman, late thirties maybe, no glamor, a little dowdy. She said my name, and I said yes, and she apologized for disturbing me. I thought for a minute she had some item for me, or she was a fan wanting to meet me. And then she told me she was a psychic and she'd received a message for me. 'I don't know whether you believe in these things,' she said, all apologetic and polite, 'and I don't want to take up your time or bother you. I've just come to Los Angeles and I don't know anyone here, but I was given your name and I found the address in the phone book.' Well, that was neither here nor there, but to save time and get rid of her I asked what the message was." Maggie Mason put out her cigarette, took another, but didn't light it immediately. "And she told me this. She said the night before she'd been meditating when two spirits—people on the other side—came to her. She described the man as being tall and bald, with a small scar on his left cheek, and he wore a Masonic ring. The woman was short and rather plump, with auburn hair in a big knot, she had very pretty slim white hands, and she was wearing a lavender silk dress. Well, that was my father and mother to the life. My mother had died just the year before, Dad five years before that.

"I was more surprised than anything else for a minute, I suppose. I just stood and goggled at her. And then she told me, still so quiet and polite, that she knew they were my parents, they told her that, and my father had said to tell me he still watched over his little Muggsy. And my mother told her my full name, and that she was to tell me that she was so pleased I had chosen the lavender silk for the funeral, she went so quickly there hadn't been a chance to tell me she wanted that, but I had known she would. But the most important part of the message was that I should be very careful in my car for the next week, to use extra caution."

She lit the cigarette. "Like most people, Mr. Falkenstein, I'm a little interested in the psychic scene. Don't know too much about it. I know there are some fake mediums around, and a lot of people who just think they've got ESP—and a few who really do have. But I'd never come across anything like that before, and I was flabbergasted. Muggsy was what my father always called me. My mother's favorite color was lavender. She was buried in the lavender silk dress. Her heart wasn't too good but she hadn't been ill—she had a heart attack and was gone in twenty-four hours. They were just ordinary people, Dad was a sixth-grade teacher, they lived very quietly, hadn't too many friends. I was an only child. And I knew that nobody except my husband and my two oldest friends knew about that Muggsy nickname."

"It impressed you," said Jesse. "No wonder."

"My God, it did. I had to believe her. She just said she'd had to come and tell me, she was sorry to have bothered me. She started down the hall, and I was the one who yanked her back and asked her name and address. She seemed a little reluctant to tell me, but she did, and admitted that she gave private sittings."

"'*Oh, wicked imagination, whence camest thou in to cover the earth with deceit?*' I do like that," said Jesse. "Very artistic."

She looked at him suspiciously. "What's that quoted from?"

"Old Rabbi Jeshu ben Sirah. You were impressed, and you mentioned this gifted seer in your column."

"I was even more impressed when I nearly got squashed on the freeway three days later, when a big semi jacknifed. That's right. The pay-off didn't happen until a year later, after I'd retired from the paper."

"What was it?"

"It was a thousand to one I ever heard about it. I hadn't been back to the neighborhood where I grew up since Dad died and we'd taken Mother to live with us. But just by chance I was in the Farmers' Market one day, and ran into old Mrs. Colson. She lived next door to us on Drexel for as long as I could remember, she knew Dad and Mother well. They'd lived there all their married life, in fact they were living there when I was born. And as Mrs. Colson and I were exchanging the amenities," said Maggie Mason grimly, "she asked me whether that nice friend of Mother's had come to see me—a very pleasant woman, stopped by way last year and was so sorry to hear they were both gone, she'd known them well some years back. They'd had a nice little chat about the old days. Well, of course I asked her, and she described Sabrina to a T. You see what the damned woman had done? One look at my birth certificate gave her the address—me the native Angeleno—but of course she was damned lucky. She didn't have to do much work on it at all, because we hadn't moved around. It wouldn't have been hard to get Mrs. Colson talking—'Was Mrs. McKechnie's hair still the same?—had Mr. McKechnie gained much weight—' Knowing Mrs. Colson, she just rambled on. And of course she knew about that nickname. The woman was damn lucky to get it all in one try."

"If she hadn't, she'd have gone on looking. There's the County Directory, Who's Who, other old neighbors if you had moved around. All sorts of ways. But she was lucky," agreed Jesse. "And I suppose it was then it occurred to you that about the easiest prediction to make to anybody living in and around L.A. is, be careful in traffic, you may have an accident."

"My God, didn't it! How many times a week does any of us have a close call? I'd just been so bemused at those accurate descriptions. It made me so damn mad, to think how I'd been had—and I couldn't even expose her—"

"Yes, you'd given her a nice send-off. Probably that brought a little handful of clients right off, and one told another."

"She's still operating here? God. When I think—taken in like a bloody five-year-old."

Jesse laughed and stood up. "I know how you feel. But don't leap to the conclusion that there aren't any genuine psychics. It's just a damn sin and shame that the Madame Sabrinas still flourish."

"But to go to the trouble—all the trouble she might have had to take, to find out—"

"Yes. Two counts," said Jesse. "Any trouble was worth the taking, when she ended up with that nice public testimonial. And the Steeles—essentially, you know, they're running a con game, and any cop could tell you that the loot is kind of secondary to the real con men. It's the game they get the kick out of."

He got back to his office at a quarter to four. The Gordons had a little news for him. Jean had finally located Mrs. Charlene Shellabarger. "I suppose I could be arrested for it, I claimed to be with Social Security checking underpayments. Everybody was very helpful." Mrs. Shellabarger was at the Shady Hills Rest Home in Tujunga. The evening visiting hours were seven to nine. And Sergeant Clock had called and dictated the record Jesse wanted.

Jesse glanced at it. The arrest of Ruth Clark at the Santa Ynez address had been her second, for narco possession and accessory to selling. She'd got ninety days, was now off probation, and the last address the L.A.P.D. had was in South Pasadena.

Nothing had been heard from the private eye in Chicago.

Jesse said resignedly he probably just had time to check the South Pasadena address. He seemed to be doing nothing but driving these days.

The South Pasadena address was a sleazy run-down old court with a strip of dry grass down the middle. The right rear unit didn't have a name on the mailbox, and he got no answer to the door; but a mountainous black woman answered the bell next door and said amiably, "Yessir, Ruth Clark, thass where she lives all right. An' her boy friend. He's a sax man with a combo, they won't get back till two, three. But she's usual here in the mornings, if you can wake her up."

He'd got used to going around in circles on this thing. Driving home, he thought he'd been ready to say the hell with it yesterday. Before he'd heard about that clock.

"Oh, my goodness, Mr. Falkenstein, you have brought back some memories to me. I only hope I'm not boring you to death. I don't have many visitors, of course the church people are nice and the minister comes now and then, but it's done me good, having somebody to talk to."

"You'd never bore anybody, Mrs. Shellabarger." If he seemed to be spending a lot of time listening to women ramble on over this business, he was pleased to have met Charlene Shellabarger. She twinkled up at him from her wheel chair, her sparse white hair a little untidy, but her skin still soft and white, her blue eyes bright. She was getting on for eighty, she'd told him, and the arthritis was a nuisance, but she'd lived with it for twenty-five years and at least her mind was as good as ever. This looked like a nice enough place for a rest home, clean and spacious. She was lucky, she said, that her Harry had made enough money—he'd had his own jewelry store in Beverly Hills—to leave her well off.

Jesse hadn't had to give much of an excuse to get her started. A little cloud on the title of the house Louise Tredgold had owned. He had nudged her into reminiscences, and she talked readily.

The old neighborhood— "Seems funny to think, most of us who bought houses there in the early days paid nine, ten thousand—a lot of money then—heaven's sake, I got a hundred and thirty thousand when I sold. After Harry went, and I had to come here. The block changed some, but four or five families stayed on for years. Raised children there. Harry and I never had any, worse luck. Some nice people came in later, a lot later—the Palfreys, the Werners, the Walshes—not getting out much, I guess I noticed more what was going on right there. My bedroom was in front, the side next to Lou Tredgold's house, and I used to just sit there a lot, looking out, seeing people come and go."

Louise— "Such a nice woman, a real friend even if she was a good bit younger. It was hard for me to get around even then, I didn't get out at all—my Harry always so good, he wanted to get a nurse, but I said the longer I could do for myself the better it'd be for me. Lou used to come in once or twice a week. It was a terrible thing, that, her getting killed. She was such a happy person, you know."

"I've seen a picture of her. She was still pretty good-looking, wasn't she? Maybe surprising she hadn't got married again. Was there ever any idea she might?"

Mrs. Shellabarger reached for her glass on the little table; her gnarled crooked hand trembled, and Jesse held it for her. "Not that I ever heard, but you're right—she was still a young woman—and you saying that, you just put me in mind of something I teased her about—and now I come to think, it was the last week of her life, too. It's a strange thing, Lou being so much younger than me—nearly fourteen years younger—and she's gone and I'm still here. That was such a terrible thing to happen, that nephew of hers—and she thought the world and all of those boys. But what was I—oh yes, the man. Her husband was dead six years, but I guess they'd been close like Harry and me. And she had the family. But now when was it, it was the Saturday night before—before she was killed—it was summer, and light till after eight, you know, and I was sitting at the bedroom window and I saw this man drive up in front, go and ring the bell, and Lou came out with him all dressed up. I did tease her about it—she dropped in to see me that Tuesday or Wednesday—and for a minute she acted kind of embarrassed, and then quick she said it was just a friend of the family come to take her to Walt's because her car wasn't working. But I wondered about it—man about her own age, kind of a tall, good-looking man with gray hair, dressed nice, good car. Only just a few days later—

"Oh, that was just an awful thing. She thought so much of those boys. Like her own, she said, and a family for Walt to leave the business to. We never knew him too well, he and Harry hadn't much in common—he was all business, day in day out—you know how there are some men, they've just got a touch for making money. That was him. A big nice-looking man, kind of what they call hearty. But when you think what they'd done for those boys—well, I guess the older one, the one named for Lou's husband, is all right.

"I remember that day like it was yesterday. You know we generally got a cool breeze at night, that near the beach, but the heat had built up and we'd left the air conditioning on all night. Harry went off about nine, and of course I didn't know it was going to be anything but an ordinary day—"

"That's a long time ago. I'll bet you don't remember much really."

"Oh, yes, I do. Nobody was coming—Mrs. Clark had been in the day before—"

"The cleaning woman. What did you think of her—nice woman?"

"Oh, I didn't see much of her, she only came once a week. She wasn't one to talk much. Nobody was coming, and it was kind of a long day. I watched the children when they came out. Not many children on the block then—the Walsh girls were getting to be young ladies, of course Bobby was kind of an afterthought, like they say. The Palfrey boy and some others were playing football in the street, in the morning. That Mike Palfrey was a caution—young daredevil. Always up to something. Later on, Mrs. Palfrey had a lot of trouble with her husband, he got to drinking and carrying on, there was a divorce and she moved away. I never minded the children playing and making noise—Lou didn't either, she often said her two—the nephews, you know—were too quiet, not like real boys—" Mrs. Shellabarger paused, lost in thought. "But Mrs. Werner, she always chased them off. She chased the boys off from playing football that morning. I got myself out to the kitchen and had the lunch Harry left. I never got in the habit of taking a nap, seems a waste of time somehow. I had a library book, but I couldn't seem to get interested in it.

"If anybody'd known what was going to happen—but of course you never do, before a thing does happen. It was just another day. The police never came to ask me anything, but of course I didn't know anything to tell them. I saw him come—that young Dick. But before that, about two o'clock, the young couple came. I'd never seen them before. They didn't stay long—"

"Young couple? They went to Mrs. Tredgold's house? You sure it was that day?"

"That's right. Girl about eighteen, and a young fellow, old beat-up car. Then they went off. A while later Mike Palfrey and a couple of other boys his age come along past the house—they had their wet bathing suits with them, they'd been up at the pool at the high school, likely. I read all about it in the papers, how the police thought it happened. I saw him come, you know. Drive up in his car. And I saw Mrs. Clark drive away, and then a little bit later he went. If I'd ever dreamed what he'd gone and done—Harry and I were having dinner when we heard the police cars— A terrible thing, and hard to believe, happening right next door." She drew a long breath, looked up at him with the ghost of a smile. "Well, ancient history—and you got me rambling on. I don't quite understand what you were saying about the title on the house, Mr. Falkenstein. I didn't mean to go talking like this. I do hope, whatever it is, you'll get it straightened out."

"So do I," said Jesse gently. "Thanks very much, Mrs. Shellabarger. Been a pleasure to meet you."

SIX

On Thursday morning Jesse was at the old court in South Pasadena at nine o'clock. Repeated assaults on the doorbell yielded no result. He pounded on the door several times; there was no sign of life within the place. He tried the doorbell again.

The door to the other half of the little ramshackle building opened and the huge black woman came out. "Man, them two night people, take something to get 'em up this hour." Helpfully she came up to shout through the front window. "Hey, Ruthie! Ruthie! Somebody to see you, honey! You from the Welfare maybe?" she asked Jesse.

"No."

"Oh. Just thought if you were, to say they're gonna get it, might help to rouse her up. Ru-thie!"

About five minutes later the door opened. "What the hell? Middle o' the night—" She was a scrawny dark girl, probably looking older than she was, yesterday's make-up creased about mouth and eyes; yawning, she showed bad teeth. "So who the hell are you?"

"I'm trying to find your mother, if she's Jean Clark."

She stared at him disgustedly. She had a frayed leopard-print terry robe tied around her, and her feet were bare; past the half-open door he could see worn linoleum, a miscellany of clothes tossed over a day bed. "How would I know where she is? We lost contact, man." She started to close the door.

"Just a minute," said Jesse sharply. "Can you tell me where your sister is then?"

"Her neither."

He straight-armed the door as it moved. "I've got a few

questions for you, Miss Clark. I'm a lawyer, and I've been doing some reinvestigating of the Tredgold case—do you remember the murder case your mother was mixed up in, had to testify in court?"

"What about it?" She was bleary-eyed, wary, but he didn't think under any drug influence. "That's crazy. That was years and years ago."

"Nevertheless, the case might be reopened. Did you ever go to see your mother at the Tredgold house, when she was working there?"

"Crazy," she said. She leaned on the doorjamb. "I got a hell of a hangover, that damn sweet wine. That place she worked so long, we were kids. The Tredgolds. Them. All that money. Well, that was one thing they couldn't buy out of, a murder—that guy they got for it—think they can get away with anything, that kind, just because they got money. Him getting that girl in trouble, they had to pay her a bundle—some people got all the luck."

"What?" said Jesse.

"Listen—" Momentarily her eyes focused on him. "I dunno who you are. I got no idea where Ma is and I could care less. She says get lost, that last bust. Hell bent to be all do-right, her and that dumb chick Amy. O.K. by me. You can get lost too." She banged the door.

The black woman had been an interested spectator. "My," she observed, "Ruthie not in a very good mood this mornin'."

Jesse wheeled and went back to the Mercedes at the curb. And just what was all that about?

Odds and ends turning up; and there was no way to know what was and what wasn't relevant. But this was a twist, all right.

Well, damn it, he had set his hand to the plow; and how many times this week had he been on the point of saying, the hell with it. This amorphous shapeless thing, nothing to be got out of it but more aimless little puzzles, bits of information that wouldn't jell—he had the dim conviction that if he could get deep enough into it, somewhere down there was something solid, some incontrovertible piece of truth.

Mostly, right now, he was feeling exasperated.

At that hour in the morning traffic wasn't bad. He took the freeway out to the exit at Pico, and went on up to Olympic.

Shopping on occasion with Nell, down the long aisles of the supermart, dropping into a market for cigarettes, it had never remotely crossed his mind to wonder about the arrangers for all that, the people sitting in offices somewhere plotting out shelf demands and discards and deliveries, staffing the supermarts so there'd be clerks and bag boys and butchers. As he spotted the address, started to hunt a parking place, he found himself thinking about it. It must take some specialized knowledge, some expert know-how.

At any rate, it didn't look like a very fancy setup. The office was on the third floor of a small brick building between a big furniture warehouse and a professional medical building. There was something called Heinsohn and Sons, Wholesale Haberdashery, on the first floor; Klein and Hertzog Pharmaceutical Supply on the second. On the top floor, the sign opposite the elevator door said simply Super-T Enterprises, with an arrow down a short hall to a frosted glass door.

Inside, there was a large square room with desks and half a dozen men at them; accountants? A little office partitioned off at the left held a middle-aged woman sitting at a typewriter, some file cases behind her. She had an unobstructed view of the door, and rose to intercept him.

"Can I help you?"

"I'd like to see Mr. Tredgold. He'll know me."

She looked at the card, and a flicker of surprise crossed her nondescript features. "Well, I'll see. He's with Smart and Final right now, and the Dairymaid agent is due in. Just take a seat, sir."

Jesse sat on a narrow vinyl chair outside the wooden railing around the desks. Typewriters clicked and banged. A fat red-faced man in tight sports clothes came out of the office beyond the woman's and bustled out. The woman came back and said, "Ralph—he wants you." A narrow-shouldered gray man in a gray suit got up from a desk and went into the inner office. About five minutes later the woman came out and said, "I think he can sandwich you in now." She led Jesse past her little cubicle to the half-open door of the inner office. There wasn't even a name on the door.

Walt Tredgold was sitting at a cluttered desk talking to the gray man, who was just nodding, holding a sheaf of accounts in one hand. It was a small office with one narrow window. "You'd better cut down the Post order by one fifth to Thousand Oaks and Sun Valley, try that for two weeks. And let me see the Dairymaid account as soon as it's posted. Thanks, Ralph." He glanced up, saw Jesse, frowned, and said, "What the hell do you want?"

"Come to rattle a family skeleton."

Tredgold passed a hand over his forehead and sat back in his desk chair. "I didn't know we had any. Millie, how about some coffee? Don't tell me you're still working for me, Falkenstein. Making bricks out of straw? Don't mind me—that last butcher in from Smart and Final was showing me an editorial out of the Santa Ana *Register*. Eighty-four per cent of all high school students convinced the greedy capitalists make at least fifty per cent profit. God. When I think how close we have to reckon—one and a half per cent norm— Don't they teach basic economics any more? Thanks, Millie. There's dairy creamer somewhere—"

Diverted, Jesse laughed. "Evidently not even the basics, and where that's going to lead us in another generation—" He sipped coffee. "Got a few questions for you. Treading on your toes."

"In what way?"

"Such as asking you about you brother getting a girl in trouble, and the family paying her off."

Walt set his cup down with a bang, spilling coffee. "And where in hell did you hear about that?" he asked quietly.

"One of Mrs. Clark's daughters came out with it."

"Now that I can't— The hell you say. I can't figure that at all. But Becky always said she snooped. I will be damned."

"Any truth in it?"

Walt looked amused and angry. "Short and sweet. Puppy-love big romance back in high school. They eloped to Vegas on graduation night. The girl was under age, and my uncle chased after them and brought them back, got the marriage annulled. The girl and her parents weren't at all averse to her marrying money, and made that pretty plain, which turned Dick off. So far as I know there certainly wasn't any question of payment involved, the girl wasn't pregnant. But I'm damned if I know how Mrs. Clark could have known about it. It was very much in the family. Oh, I suppose the girl could have talked—but there wasn't anything to it. But Mrs. Clark—"

"Yes. Mrs. Clark. Where did your aunt come by Mrs. Clark in the first place, do you know?"

"Well, yes." Tredgold drank coffee. "As it happens I do know, and I don't think I'd thought about it from that day to this." He was looking deeply angry: a man who spluttered over little things, only rarely felt great anger. "Damn it, I never thought twice about the woman, I never looked at her—she was a fixture, just there, the cleaning woman. And then she knifed Dick in the back like that, for no reason. She'd had nothing but kindness, a good job, from Aunt Lou. Yes, I can tell you. It was Uncle Walt. When the hell?—I was about second or third year at U.S.C., Dick was still in high school. There were domestics came and went, I don't remember any of them —women to do the cleaning, nobody regular, I mean there was never a cook, Aunt Lou did all that, but women to help. Uncle Walt said something at dinner one night—this woman, some connection of an old employee, down on her luck, find a job for her."

"Well." Jesse contemplated that and made nothing of it.

"I don't think I ever consciously noticed the woman. Of course I wasn't at the house, usually, when she was there. A couple of years later Becky and I were married and had our own place. Ah, damn it, just as she said, raking it all up again.

Bringing it all back. What in hell did that damned woman have against Dick?"

"After the murder," asked Jesse, "did she go on working at the house—awhile, that is? Help in cleaning it up, after the police were finished there? You didn't know then she was going to do any knifing, I suppose."

"No," said Walt tersely. "She never came back at all. When the police wanted to talk to her, I couldn't tell them her address, I think they got it from some other woman there she'd worked for."

"Oh. A little something else." Jesse wasn't about to break the news of the elusive boy friend to him. "Can you think of any family friend about sixty-five now, tall, gray-haired, nice-looking?"

Walt just looked at him. "You said something about busy-work. Don't. About the only fellow that age we know is Becky's father, and he's been bald ever since I knew him. What the hell are you playing at?"

Jesse didn't have to ask what he'd think about that clock.

At loose ends, he went back to Hollywood and up to his office. There wasn't anything in from the private eye in Chicago. "Have you enjoyed yourself, goofing off?" asked Jean. "Flu's not supposed to last more than three days. You've had nine calls yesterday and today. You may be interested to know that on Monday a Mr. Wagner called from Truax Construction, and I turned him down, and in this morning's papers they're suing a builders' supply company for half a million. Douglas and Potter are representing."

"Yes, a pity," said Jesse. He wandered into his office and sat down, leaving the door open. He thought, if he were to tell the whole story to the Gordons they'd probably be interested, but being very practical females would tell him there was nowhere to go on it and he'd better stop wasting his time.

He wondered what old Edgar would have said about it, and conjured up a vision of the old man, portly and red-faced, there in the corner, with the inevitable bulge of the bottle in his breast pocket. The old man, he remembered suddenly, who had also parlayed some luck and business shrewdness into an independent fortune, and would have sympathized with the Tredgolds, all that legal tangle over the will when Dick was found guilty of the murder.

And he would have been interested in that clock.

Jimmy looked into the office. "Should I send out for some lunch, Mr. Falkenstein?"

"Oh—don't bother. I'll sit on the phone if you want to go together." Wasting time like this. Time being money. All the clients turned away.

He was still sitting there, staring absently at the rather grim portrait of Sir Thomas More, when the Gordons came back. But twenty minutes later he got up and went out, avoiding their severe looks.

This time he sought out the former landlady on Berendo Avenue, and asked her about Mrs. Clark's daughter. "Was it the older one who got married?"

"That's right, before Mrs. Clark moved away. Married a fellow she went to school with, Jim Smith."

Something within Jesse protested strongly; there should be a limit to the obstacles life set a man. "You wouldn't know where they're living?"

"Goodness, now. That was four, five years back. I think his father had a Shell station, I remember that, he worked there."

A very small light in the darkness? When the two had gone to school together, the Smiths must have lived in this school district; it was possible the Shell station was somewhere fairly close, but there wasn't any certainty about that at all. Jesse retired to a phone booth and consulted the listing of service stations in the yellow pages. There were a lot of Shell stations, all over the place, and nothing said that Smith still had the franchise on one of them. There were also quite a few Smiths. He found out on the first try that he couldn't check by phone; trying to explain to a busy mechanic that he was looking for a Jim Smith who'd married a girl named Clark was impossible. There were eleven possible Shell stations, from the Atwater district to Vernon and in between, and it took time to check them all.

He reflected bitterly, pulling into the seventh one, that he now knew what Andrew meant when he said the worst part of the thankless job was the interminable legwork.

Here, however, he struck lucky. A rather stupid-looking but amiable blond youth came to him and admitted that he was Jim Smith. Yeah, his wife's name had been Clark. He stared at Jesse. "Praise heaven," said Jesse. "I'm trying to locate your mother-in-law."

"Oh, her. Why?"

"Just some little business to do with her last job. Forms to sign. Do you know where she's living?"

"Nope, but Amy'll know, you could ask her." He wasn't curious, didn't ask how Jesse had been led to him; there were bureaucratic forms to sign all over the place these days. He gave Jesse the address readily: Serrano Place.

It was one side of a shabby frame duplex, and the girl who came to the door had a baby in one arm and a yelling two-year-old on the floor behind her. She looked as amiable and slightly stupid as her husband, a vapidly pretty dark girl with cowlike brown eyes.

"Ma?" she said. "Oh, sure I can tell you. She's working at a rest home down in Hawthorne, she lives on 110th." She brought an address book and showed him, and he copied it down.

"Do you remember when your mother worked for Mrs. Tredgold?"

She looked blank, hushing the baby, and then said, "Oh, that place she worked so long. She got awful good money there. That was the lady that had such beautiful clothes, she'd give some to Ma now and then, but of course they were too old for Ruth and me then and Ma wouldn't wear them, she used to sell them secondhand."

"Did you ever go to see her there? To the house?"

"She took us all through it once. The lady went to Hawaii and Ma let us see the house while she was gone. Gee, it was a beautiful place—all the expensive furniture and velvet drapes and all. But that was the place—"

"Did you ever go there again, maybe you and Jim—before you were married—or with another boy friend? One afternoon?"

She thought. "I kind of remember that. Yeah, it was Jim. He was broke and we wanted to go to a show. I got him to drive me there so I could ask Ma for some money. That was the place there was the murder—I sure remember *that*, and how Ma had to testify in court."

"Yes. Well, thanks for the address." Jesse was annoyed again. Whenever he turned up anything apparently new on this case, almost immediately it dissolved into meaninglessness. And very probably, in eight years, Amy had changed enough that Mrs. Shellabarger couldn't identify her anyway.

He went home early and annoyed Nell by hanging around while she was trying a new recipe for beef stroganoff. "For heaven's sake go and listen to Bach or something, Jesse. I can't listen to you and measure things at the same time. I'll hear all about it at dinner."

David Andrew was peacefully asleep. Jesse regarded him with absent fondness, hoping he wouldn't carry on the family tradition and grow up to be a lawyer. He wondered what his father would think about this damned shapeless case—it wasn't enough of anything to be a case. Unfortunately, Falkenstein Senior was in Sacramento with a dozen other corporation lawyers, giving testimony to a Senate subcommittee.

The beef stroganoff having arrived at a successful conclusion, Nell listened to the story of his day, "I must say," she observed, "that woman is more and more of an enigma, Jesse. That's something new—she didn't come out of a want ad or an employment bureau. Uncle Walt brought her home. Relative of faithful employee down on her luck."

"Now don't try to tell me she was an ex-girl friend," said Jesse. "Hardly the way you'd pay one off. He doesn't seem to have been the type anyway. All business. It's likely that was just the bare fact, him being kind and helping somebody out. Everybody said she was a good reliable worker. Worth what they paid her."

"And then turning to bite the hand that fed her. I haven't heard any compliments on the stroganoff."

"Oh, very nice indeed—very good. You're worth your hire too. You like to come with me to see this female?"

Nell laughed. "I might inhibit your questioning."

"But, damn it, I'm still curious about the boy friend. That must have been him Mrs. Shellabarger saw, when Walt didn't recognize the description. Of course he couldn't have anything to do with the murder—"

"How do you know? I'll agree with Mrs. Tredgold—no one can be sure of exact times. Mrs. Werner could have gone in the house earlier. Mrs. Shellabarger could have dozed off, missed seeing someone else go in after Dick left. I'd like to know about the boy friend too," said Nell thoughtfully.

She was stacking dishes in the dishwasher and Jesse was putting his tie back on when the baby woke up and demanded instant attention. "I'll be back some time," said Jesse, looking into the nursery, and she waved a dirty diaper at him. In the front hall he nearly collided with his sister Fran.

"Don't you people know enough to lock doors after dark? I just walked around after another book for Andrew." The Clocks lived just around the corner on Hillcrest Road. "He's got into the *ESP Reader* now—very clever of you to hand him the good popular-written stuff, Jesse—and I think the best thing to give him next is that Alson J. Smith book, if you can lay your hands on it."

"Alphabetical listing, left-hand bookcase in the den," said Jesse. "I'll see you later."

This wasn't the oldest section of L.A., but it was one of the dreariest, consisting of much small manufacturing, blocks of warehouses, near-slum residential streets, wholesale business. The address he had from Amy turned out to be a rectangular box of an apartment building, jerry-built probably within the last five years and the paint already peeling, graffiti on all the walls, the elevators unpredictable. He rode up to the seventh floor.

The hall was narrow, the walls thin by the various echoes from within. The door he wanted was labeled 720; there wasn't a bell or a knocker. He used his knuckles.

There was sudden movement within, and in five seconds the door opened. And here was Jean Clark: the woman of the gratuitous lies on the witness stand, the knifer in the back, the enigma. She looked to Jesse like a very ordinary woman, not even a very intelligent woman. She was short and solid and square, a lump of a woman. She had a sallow roundish face with small dark eyes sunk in the flesh, no eyebrows, a thin-lipped too-small mouth, and her still black hair was scraped back from her face into a hard knot at the back. She had on a drab brown bathrobe and frayed terry-cloth slippers.

Jesse didn't waste any time. He handed her a card. "You remember the Tredgold case, Mrs. Clark. The murder of Mrs. Louise Tredgold, while you were working for her. Maybe it's all going to be brought up again. Because not everything came out at the time, did it? You told a few lies on the witness stand, and that amounts to perjury."

She stared at him. She wasn't rattled at all; maybe her mind moved slowly. She said, "That couldn't be, not after all this time. I never told any lies and there's no way anybody could prove I did." She had a rather harsh loud voice, flat.

"What did you have against the Tredgold family, anyway?" he asked conversationally. "Mrs. Tredgold had given you a good job, paid you well. You'd been with her for a long time. You testified that you liked her, she was a generous and considerate employer."

"That's right. She was. I don't see any reason to waste time, talk it all over. It was over with years back. What are you after anyways?" She stood there solid and unyielding, not leaning on the door, and her little eyes were hard as stones on him.

"But I told you, maybe it's all going to be raked up again, Mrs. Clark. How did you find out about Dick Tredgold's elopement?"

Her face changed, some expression flashed across it and was gone. "Where'd you hear that?" she asked sharply.

"Why, from your daughter Ruth."

Her mouth tightened. "Little whore," she said. "I tried best I knew how, bring up the girls straight and honest—it wasn't so easy, a woman alone, not much money—nobody can say it's my fault Ruth went wrong. Taking up with the riffraff, getting into the dope. I told her I never wanted see her again, and I don't. I'd forgot I ever mentioned that." She looked at him now with sour amusement. "I was just the cleaning girl," she said. "Sometimes Mis' Tredgold had the rest of them for dinner, I'd stay to clean up. They'd talk—I couldn't help but hear."

"I see," said Jesse. "But just what did you have against Dick Tredgold, to tell those lies in court?"

"Mister," she said flatly, "I don't know what game you're tryin' to play, all that's over 'n' done, but if they bring it all up again all I can say is what I said before. I was tired that day and why should I take much notice of what they was up to? I said what I saw and what I didn't see. I'd washed all the side and back windows of that house that day, I was beat and I wanted to get home. And I don't have to answer any questions or stand here wasting time with you." She stepped back and shut the door with a little thud.

Jesse paced thoughtfully back to the elevator. As he'd thought, reading the transcript, an obstinate, pigheaded witness you couldn't coax or lead. She'd stick to the tale that black was white unless you could prove in spades she was a liar. But there was something he couldn't put a finger on there too—some little thing at the back of his mind, not quite right.

When he turned into the drive of the house on Rockledge Road and went in the back door, he found Fran still there. "I've been hearing all about your ancient murder. What was the chief witness like, now you've found her?"

"Very much what I expected. And again, not exactly." Jesse went to get himself a drink. The girls had been having more coffee, and cookies sat on a plate between them, guarded from Athelstane, who leaned hopefully against Fran's legs.

"I'm afraid there's only one answer," said Fran as Jesse came back with the drink. "For once your instinct's wrong and he's guilty after all."

"You didn't tell her about the clock." Jesse had brought a bowl of cocktail pretzels with him and instantly Athelstane abandoned Fran to lean on him.

Fran was entranced with the clock. "That really clinches it, doesn't it? She was murdered after he left. But I really don't see how, Jesse. It was a locked room, in a way. Every direction covered."

"I'm not sure," said Nell. "And the more I think about the boy friend, the more I think he could be the dark horse."

"Oh yes, I'd like to find him," agreed Jesse, slipping pretzels to Athelstane absently. "But she was so damn discreet. Probably for the reasons you deduced, Nell. But when she was so cautious she didn't mention anything definite even to her nearest friends, and there wasn't any known connection between them, evidently— Either of you have any brilliant suggestions where to look?" Nell shook her head.

"Certainly," said Fran calmly. He looked at her suspiciously: slim, small, svelte Fran, looking as usual more like a magazine-cover model, in scarlet turtleneck and black pants, than a cop's wife. "You forget I know about women, dear. Their foibles." Until she turned into a cop's wife, Fran had been editor of a fashion magazine. "Find her hairdresser."

"What?" said Jesse.

"I never thought of that!" said Nell.

"Of course not, darling." Fran smiled at her affectionately. "You being the one woman in a thousand can get by with wearing it like that, just the plain big chignon, you don't patronize beauty salons. But I'd take a large bet that Louise did. Faithfully. And it's a very funny thing, but women will often tell the girl fussing around their hair things they wouldn't come out with to their closest friends. It's psychological."

"In what way?" asked Jesse.

"Well, for one thing, the girl doing their hair is an outsider. She'll never meet any of the family or friends they're talking about. So they feel safe. It's rather like a man talking to a bartender," said Fran. "And especially they'll get to talking if they go to the same one every week. It's only Liz, or Ann, or Linda, nobody who matters. But I'd add a qualification."

"Which is?"

"Well, if she knew any of her close friends went to the same place, she probably wouldn't talk as freely. But if you want my considered opinion, she talked to somebody," said Fran. Nell looked amused.

"Why?" asked Jesse.

"Oh, darling. I don't care what the circumstances are," said Fran, "or how old the woman is—or how young—that doesn't enter in. But any woman at all, any place in the world any time, if she's attracted a man who looks serious about her—she's got to talk about him to somebody. She can't help it."

"Well, it's a thought," said Jesse. "I suppose you'd know. And I'd also suppose your spouse is wondering where you are. I'll walk you home—muggers can show up anywhere."

Clock had accepted the new book with a grunt. But the one he took with him on Friday morning was the first one he'd read. Some time in late morning when he and Petrovsky were alone in the squad room, he slid it across the desk and said diffidently, "Some interesting things in that."

Petrovksy glanced at it. "Oh, that. Yeah, I read it a while back."

"You did?" Clock was surprised. "I—er—didn't realize some other forces really take it seriously. Call in these psychics. The R.C.M.P., and Berlin, and Paris. Of course the hypnosis isn't quite the same thing." Along with many other forces, these days, the L.A.P.D. was finding hypnosis very useful for prodding the memories of friendly witnesses.

Petrovsky's round snub-nosed face turned thoughtfully to the copy of *Crime and the Psychic World.* "Yeah," he said. "By the record, maybe we ought to have a fling at it, in certain cases. If there are any reliable psychics around here. It's not evidence, but sometimes it can point where to look for evidence."

———

Once more Jesse surprised a Tredgold with an unexpected question. "What on earth—" said Becky. "I'm beginning to think Ray Austin underestimated you. Well, the one at Robinsons' in Beverly Hills. I won't ask why you want to know."

"Did you go there too? Know if any of her friends did?"

"I don't, no, and never did. I don't know about her friends."

"Well, thanks."

It hadn't occurred to him until he got there what an awkward place for a lone male it would be. The anteroom of Nikki's Beauty Salon, high up in Robinsons' department store, was lushly carpeted; there was a certain hush, with muted voices and mysterious sounds in the background, and heavy scents on the air. A few women sat about in flame-colored chairs, waiting. And around three sides of the place rows of faceless heads wearing exquisitely coifed wigs made him nervous. There was a highly polished brunette sitting at a tiny desk, who surveyed him coldly with superciliously raised brows.

"Somebody who was here eight years ago?" she repeated. "May I enquire why?"

Jesse had settled on an economical answer. "One of your regular customers then got herself murdered. I'm writing a book about the case."

The brunette turned human at once. "My God, you don't mean Mrs. Tredgold? That one? Well, I'll be—" She was excited and interested. "Do I remember that! One of our regulars —and a nice woman. I'll be darned. What do you want to know?"

"Well, which of the girls usually did her hair. Did she have the same one most of the time?"

"Oh, sure. Sure she did. Pat. Most of the same girls were

here then, I've been here ten years myself. What'll Pat say! A book!"

"This Pat, she on today?"

"No, it's her day off. Pat Logan. But say, I can give you her address, and I'll be glad to give her a ring, tell her you're coming to see her. She just lives in Santa Monica. I know she shops in the morning, she ought to be home by one. Gee, I can't get over it—"

"I'd be obliged," said Jesse. He took the address and escaped with relief from the eyeless heads, no less than from the brunette's avid gaze.

And there was another little idea he wanted to check on, just for his own satisfaction. As per Maggie Mason's experience. He remembered that Celia Adams had said Lou hadn't had a real message until the second session with Sabrina. Which figured. Somebody checking the contents of handbags for names, addresses, any useful hints. Somebody, possibly, calling unobtrusively at a house a couple of doors away, insurance agent with innocent questions. Likely the first thing turned up would have been, widow of Walter Tredgold, owner of big market chain. And there would have been an obituary in the L.A. *Times*.

He wanted to see exactly what meat there might have been in that for Sabrina.

He drove down to the big *Times-Mirror* building and consulted the directory in the lobby. The morgue was appropriately in the basement. Unlike the busy, bustling first floor it was hushed as a library, rather ghostly, with one attendant barely visible behind stacks of file cases. When he attracted her attention she drifted toward him helpfully. Jesse told her what he was after, the year. "Don't know the date, sorry."

"I can probably find it. We're all cross-filed." She drifted away. Less than five minutes later she came back with a mock-up page. "There's a copier by the door, if you need any."

The first thing he looked at with interest was the picture. Walter Tredgold had been not exactly handsome, but it was a face of strong character: a large prow of a nose, stubborn jaw, wide-spaced eyes under heavy tufted brows. He wore square-shaped dark-rimmed glasses. He looked like a man who knew his own mind, would stand for no nonsense, He was also the picture of the successful man, embodiment of the American dream.

The dateline was Los Angeles, March 3. "Walter Fitzpatrick Tredgold, fifty-nine, died yesterday of a massive coronary occlusion. The attack occurred in his private office at Super-T Enterprises in Santa Monica. Given emergency treatment by paramedics, Mr. Tredgold was taken by ambulance to St. John's Hospital, where he was pronounced dead on arrival.

"Mr. Tredgold was the owner and sole proprietor of Super-T Enterprises, a chain of supermarkets which had grown from one small independent grocery to comprise twenty-one large supermarts throughout the Los Angeles area. Speaking at a banquet of the National Association of American Businessmen last year, Mr. Tredgold stated, 'Part of success in business is luck, part is simply the application of sound business management principles, but the greater part always lies in hard, unremitting work.'

"Applying this principle in his own career, Tredgold began his remarkable rise in entrepreneurship over thirty years ago, when he opened a grocery store on Lincoln Avenue in Santa Monica with only his wife and one employee as assistants. Three years later he was able, although still having the liability of a mortgage on his first store, to open a second small market in West Los Angeles. This enterprise failed a year later when a disastrous fire caused by defective wiring swept through the building causing virtually total loss. Fortunately insurance covered the major part of the loss and in ensuing years Tredgold incorporated his growing chain of markets under the name of Super-T. Last year it was estimated that the corporation showed gross sales of just under seven million dollars.

"Tregold was active in the Rotary Club, the National Association of American Businessmen, and had been chairman of the Community Chest and United Way in past years. He was known for his generous contributions to various charities.

"Mr. Tredgold and his wife, Louise, who had no children, had adopted the two sons of Tredgold's brother, Dr. Charles Tredgold, after he and his wife were killed in the crash of a DC-3 en route to San Francisco. It is presumed that control of the Super-T Enterprises will be retained by the family.

"Funeral arrangements are pending and will be private."

Jesse looked at this with something less than enthusiasm. It would have offered Sabrina some meat. But enough?

And what did it matter?

SEVEN

"The funny thing is," said Pat Logan, "I was just thinking about Mrs. Tredgold the other day—couldn't say why, she just came into my mind. And then you turning up to ask about her —it's funny." She had at first looked a little disappointed in him; obviously, to Pat Logan, an Author who Wrote Books should have some distinguishing mark, such as two heads. "Ever since Marge called, I've been thinking back, everything I could remember about Mrs. Tredgold. What do you want to know, Mr. Falkenstein?"

"Well, suppose you tell me some of what you remember, and I'll think of some questions."

"Well, she was a nice woman. I've worked at Nikki's for nearly eighteen years, and Mrs. Tredgold had been coming regular, I'd done her every week for ten years anyway. She was one of my nicest ladies, she always tipped well, but I mean she was friendly too. She always asked about the kids— we've got two—and how my hay fever was. Well, you know, friendly."

Pat Logan was a large blonde about forty-five, with a beautiful pink and white complexion. The living room of this old frame bungalow on a quiet street was shadowy, crowded with miscellaneous furniture. She sat on the edge of the couch, watching him eagerly, "What should I tell you? She was just nice. We couldn't believe it, her getting killed like that. I know she'd just been in the day before."

"She was coming to you," said Jesse, "when her husband died."

"Oh yes, that was awful too, it was so sudden—he died before she could get to him, she was all broken up over it. They'd been married thirty years."

"I don't want to put any ideas in your mind," said Jesse cautiously. "That was six years before. There hadn't been any indication, after that, that she was, well, interested in any other man—but I've come across a few little signs that just before the murder she may have been. I wonder if she'd dropped any hints to you that she had a new man friend, might be thinking—" He paused hopefully.

The blue eyes widened on him. "But if that isn't just what I said to Marge when she called! You must be using ESP, Mr. Falkenstein. She *was*. She sure had. The first idea I got of it— like I say I've been thinking back to know what to tell you, after Marge called—it was about a month before the murder. She'd come in, and it was after I'd combed her out, she sort of leaned to the mirror and said, 'I don't really look my age, do I?' and I said she sure didn't. And she really didn't, you know—she was a real pretty woman. And she smiled and said, life in the old girl yet, and I said kind of joking maybe she had a new romance, and she said maybe. And the week after when she came in I said how's the romance coming, kidding you know, but she was kind of serious, it was real strange, I forget exactly how she put it but it was what she meant, she'd thought everything was settled how it'd be the rest of her life, but it looked as if it'd all change and a new life start all over. She asked did I think she was too old to get married again, and of course I said no."

Jesse hardly felt surprised. His little sister Fran usually knew what she was talking about. "Did she tell you the man's name, anything about him?"

"Not much, Mr. Falkenstein. Naturally I wasn't going to ask questions. If she wanted to tell me things, that was different. She was kind of shy about it, like—well, almost like a girl with her first boy—it was sort of touching, know what I mean. She said she was nervous about her family, about telling them, she hoped they wouldn't think she was making a mistake, especially on top of that other thing—"

"Her interest in the medium," said Jesse.

"Oh, you know about that? Yes, she'd told me a lot about that, it was awfully interesting. Do you know, Mr. Falkenstein, her husband had come back, that medium gave her all sorts of messages from him, things the medium couldn't possibly have known, he remembered their anniversary and the nephews' birthdays and things about his will and the business, and she said some little things like the trouble with his new car and the emerald ring he gave her on her last birthday, nobody knew outside the family. It was wonderful. But the family just wouldn't believe it. And she was afraid they'd disapprove of her taking up with this man too. Though she said he was a real gentleman, there wasn't any reason they should disapprove, he had plenty of money and all."

"Didn't she tell you anything definite about him at all?"

"I thought afterward, it kind of made it worse—when maybe she was going to start a whole new life. Well, the only thing she said was kind of funny," said Pat Logan. "She said one reason the family might not like it was that they hadn't been properly introduced. She sort of giggled about that. She said, it was a real pickup. She'd met him at the auto agency where they were both waiting for their cars to be fixed up."

Clock came back from lunch about one o'clock and found an autopsy report waiting on his desk. He wasn't much interested in it. Petrovsky was out talking to people on the latest arson, and the squad room was empty. He sat there for ten minutes, and finally he opened the top drawer and said aloud, "God-damnit! For what it's worth—" He took out the suicide note.

There had been casual references, now and then, to Jesse's spook factory; he didn't quite remember the name, Western something, but thought he'd recognize it in the phone book. He did. It was a fifteen-minute drive: Santa Monica Boulevard.

He passed Johnny Mantella downstairs, but just gave him a nod.

It didn't look very fancy: a set of offices on the third floor of an old building. He went in the door, and there was a very plain girl sitting at a desk, and a man. There was something familiar about both of them. The man, a tall dark lean fellow in his forties, looked up and said urbanely, "Sergeant Clock," and something clicked in Clock's mind. That homicide case, client of Jesse's getting murdered: these people had both been witnesses. The man was DeWitt.

"Er—yes," said Clock.

"Can we do something for you?" asked DeWitt politely, after a moment.

"Well," said Clock rather defiantly, "yes. I'd like to see this MacDonald fellow."

"You mean, for a consultation?" DeWitt seldom showed surprise. "It's not one of his regular days here, Sergeant, but as a matter of fact he is here, looking over some files. But it's his lunch hour, I don't know—"

"Lunch hour?"

"Why, yes, he works for the city as an electrician, you know."

Clock hadn't known. "I'd like to see him if he's got time," he said brusquely.

DeWitt said, "I'll see." He went into the next office and in half a minute came back. "You can come in here."

"Er—is there a charge?"

"A donation if you like, seeing that your brother-in-law's on the board." DeWitt was grave. Clock fished out a five-dollar bill.

The room was just a room, furnished as a study and not large. There was a couch, small coffee table, a couple of armchairs. Sitting on the couch was a thin-faced man with thick dark hair and dark eyes. He was dressed in ordinary tan work clothes. He looked at Clock and said, "I haven't got much time, I'm sorry—I'm due back on the job. Ten minutes?"

Clock sat down opposite him, feeling obscurely guilty. MacDonald didn't know him from Adam. But when that queer frame had been set up on him, and things had looked pretty hopeless, Fran had come to this man and he'd given them one little clue that had led the old man to the truth, and cleared Clock. And he felt now that he might have had the decency to come and thank him.

"I'd better tell you what I'm after," he said bluntly. "Just see if you can tell me any little thing." He handed over Milton Peters' suicide note, folded. "This man is dead. We can't find his body."

"Ah," said MacDonald. He took the page and held it between his palms, looking down at it. After twenty seconds he said suddenly, "Oh, he grew up in the country—lots of trees, green meadows—he always wanted to go back. Barns, there are barns. He was in such despair—such awful loneliness, and so tired—he wanted to go back. Barns, barns, barns—I don't know why I see that, but it's what comes through—barns and stalls, barns and stalls, barns and stalls—" The words were slurred together rapidly.

And two seconds later they fused in Clock's mind and he sprang to his feet. "My good God almighty!" he said. "Barnsdall Park! Barnsdall Park!" And he ran out through the anteroom and down the stairs without waiting for the elevator.

MacDonald came to the anteroom door. "I seem to have said something."

DeWitt blinked at him, adjusting his glasses. "You frequently do, Charles."

But Clock was intent on the job. Back at the precinct, he told the desk sergeant to have a couple of traffic units on standby and plunged upstairs to find Petrovsky just in, as he'd hoped. Rapidly he sketched it for him—"Like magic, Pete, and it just slid into my mind what he was saying—the guy may be a hundred per cent wrong, but I just saw it—we never thought Peters had done it somewhere outside, because for one thing it was raining like hell most of that week. But Barnsdall Park—this time of year—"

"Maybe the psychic just rang a loud bell," agreed Petrovsky. "We can go look."

Barnsdall Park was a queer oasis in the middle of busy city

streets: a large square block, rising to a hill, between Sunset and Hollywood boulevards, Edgemont and Vermont avenues. There was an art gallery at the top of the hill, and picnic areas, playgrounds for the kids; it was thickly wooded with old olive and California oak trees. In summer it got a fair amount of people, though it wasn't as popular as some other parks; at this time of year it would be deserted, except for the part-time staff of the art gallery.

They went up there with two traffic units. "How would he get here?" asked Petrovsky.

"Bus up Vermont," said Clock tersely. "If that's right, that he was a country boy, for all we knew he had a habit of coming up here, to sit under the trees." But once there, with his game leg, there weren't many places he could have gone. It would have been a tough pull for him up the hill.

About three quarters of the way up, off to one side of the path, was a little clearing with some swings, a table, and a couple of benches. That was where they found Milton Peters, half hidden behind a big oak tree, sitting up against it. His shabby suit was still sodden with rain, and the little .22 revolver was still under his right hand.

"Now I will be goddamned!" said Clock. "I will be goddamned! Just like that he said it—barns and stalls—just feeling that note!"

"Very helpful," said Petrovsky. One of the traffic men had gone back to the squad to call up the morgue wagon. "One of the things a lot of psychics seem to be good at is finding bodies. I suppose we might have thought of the park if it had been summer."

"The fact remains we didn't," said Clock. Like most of the utter skeptics when suddenly converted, he was impressed to something like awe. "I can't get over it. Just like that he—"

"Yeah, well, at least we've got this cleared out of the way," said Petrovsky with a sniff. "What I'm worried about is this damned arsonist. Sooner or later, just by the law of averages, he's going to kill somebody. I was talking to the arson squad at headquarters when you roared in, and from looking at that contraption we picked up in the public rest room they think he's got some rudimentary knowledge of explosives. You think I'd be woolgathering to suggest we get a list of any AWOLs thought to be in the area? It's just an idea."

"Yes, I suppose," said Clock. He was still staring at Milton Peters' body.

———

Resignedly Jesse had got back to Walt Tredgold with another out-of-the-blue question. "Hope I didn't disturb you."

"I was writing to Dick." Just as resignedly Tredgold answered the question. "The Quincy Chrysler agency on San Vicente in Santa Monica. We've all dealt with them for years. Is that all you want to know?"

Jesse said meekly it was. He didn't expect much at the agency, and he didn't get much. Mr. Adam Quincy, serenely pleased to meet any friend of a friend—old Mr. Tredgold and now his nephew had been excellent customers for many years, Mr. Quincy had had the agency for thirty years—told him what he had guessed for himself. Quincy was polite on suppressing curiosity at the question, tactful in glossing over the murder. Jesse said casually it was just a small matter recently come to light, if Mr. Quincy could help them— Mr. Quincy could not. Someone Mrs. Tredgold had met casually, here at the agency, while having her car serviced? Eight years ago? He spread his hands and shrugged.

Any automobile agency had so much space for paperwork. Records on new cars and customers were kept only as long as the warranty was in effect. People bringing in older models for service, a record of the work and charge was filed until the monthly accounts were made up, and then disposed of. There was no possible way to track down, now, what dates Mrs. Tredgold had been in to have the oil changed, brakes adjusted, some other minor maintenance that would take a short enough time that she would have waited for it in the showroom.

Mr. Quincy coughed. "As a matter of fact, I happen to

remember that on the—er—day when she was killed, her car was in our garage. For the ten-thousand-mile checkup."

Which said nothing at all. Jesse swore to himself. Fran being so clever and helpful, and she'd been quite right about the hairdresser; but like every other tiny possible lead in this thing, fizzling out like a damp firecracker. Louise running into her handsome new boy friend in Mr. Quincy's elegant showroom—this much later, anybody's guess as to when, who, or why.

And it was threatening to rain again. Well, they'd been promised a wet winter, and it was long overdue.

He got back to the office at four-thirty. Jimmy said somebody named Walsh had called, would call back. "Put him through when he does," said Jesse, and sat down in his desk chair and swiveled away from the deliberate, somehow accusing gaze of Sir Thomas More. He looked out at the gray lowering clouds, which hid the line of the Hollywood hills, for five minutes, and then he swung around, consulted his address book, and picked up the phone.

Three rings, and a husky voice answered. "Sabrina Steele speaking."

"Mrs. Steele, I'd like to make an appointment for a private sitting. What is the charge?"

"Fifty dollars. I haven't a period free for several days."

"Perhaps for double the usual fee? I'm very anxious to consult you soon."

A pause. "Well, let me see. I could give you an hour at eight o'clock on Monday evening. You will please give me only an initial to identify you, whatever the guides may tell you will be all the more convincing."

At least the lady was willing, thought Jesse sardonically. Not that you could generalize, but the Madame Sabrinas infinitely preferred female clients, which was usually what they got. Most men weren't so prone to giving away clues. But she'd risk trying to feed him generalities, for a double fee, not caring if he didn't come back.

Jean looked in. "Mr. Walsh is on the line."

Jesse picked up the phone again. "Oh, good, you're there," said Bob Walsh. "First of all, I thought you'd like to know that it's doing it again. Day before yesterday and yesterday."

"The clock," said Jesse.

"That's right. Five forty-seven on the nose. I'm going to sit right here and watch it, catch it in the act today. Also, I've got a little idea. I don't know what you'll think about it, sir. But you see, I'm due to be hypnotized tomorrow afternoon—"

"What'd you say?"

"Hypnotized. It's this Experimental Psychology class—junior elective actually, but they let me in because I usually get A's across the field and scored top in college boards," said Bob unapologetically. "Part of the course is on hypnosis, and we all have to be tested and do experiments in posthypnotic effects and so on. I seem to be a pretty good subject. And I'm due for the monthly session with Dr. Fredericks tomorrow, and I had a kind of bright idea, I think."

"For instance?"

"Well, suppose he took me right back to that day? I suppose you know that a hypnotized subject can dredge up stuff his conscious mind doesn't remember at all. And for all we know, I may have some important clue buried down there," said Bob cheerfully. "After all, far as I recollect, I was hanging around that block somewhere all that day."

"It's an idea indeed," said Jesse. "What does Dr. Fredericks think?"

"Oh, he's definitely interested. I told him something about it, and you—hope you don't mind. He says it'd be an interesting experiment, and you'd be welcome to sit in. I didn't," said Bob, "tell him about the clock."

Jesse laughed. "I should think not. But just remember, Bob, there was a time not too long ago when hypnosis was lumped together by orthodox science along with fortunetellers, witches, magicians, and mediums."

"That's right, isn't it?"

"Where do I come and when?"

"I'll meet you at the front of the science building at two

o'clock. Say, I'm glad you like this idea. I was afraid—but we might get something, you know."

"We just might. Thanks, Bob, I'll see you."

———————————

When he got home, unexpectedly Nell made him a drink while he was taking off his tie, and told him to sit down. She had made herself one too. "Doubles," she said, "while I break the news to you and you digest it."

"My God," said Jesse, "you're going to have another baby?"

"Not *yet*," said Nell, looking alarmed. "No. I've found a house. Jesse, it really is a beautiful house. Just like the country. An acre, and lots of trees, and a chain-link fence all round—you know that alone would cost a fortune now. And you'll love the house, I think." She was looking at him anxiously. "It's not new. Not modern. It sort of sprawls, and there's a tile roof. Four big bedrooms, a dining room, and a great big study with built-in bookshelves on three sides."

"What's the catch? This tastes more like a triple."

"No catch really. It needs some things done to it, paint and so on, but it was all rewired three years ago and there's a new dishwasher built in. Hardwood floors. Two fireplaces. Forced-air heat and central air conditioning. Drink your drink."

Jesse looked at her with deep suspicion. "It's got a ghost?"

"Well, I hope not, but I don't think we'd mind her anyway. It belonged to a maiden lady who was a real artist and did illustrations for children's books." Athelstane was padding between them begging for pretzels. "She left it to a niece in Omaha, which is why it's for sale. There's a three-car garage and a partial basement. And an option to buy any of the furniture. It's all solid old stuff, and I thought—you know what new furniture costs, and most of it not worth the price—we'd need a good deal more to furnish it fully anyway."

"All right. Where is it?"

"It really wouldn't be *much* further for you to drive. And that's another thing. It's right at the end of a cul-de-sac road, only one other house on it a long way off, just off Coldwater Canyon."

"Go on," said Jesse after a minute.

"Well, that's about it. I thought I could take you to see it in the morning."

"Why," asked Jesse, "the triple drinks?"

"It's a hundred and eighty thousand dollars," said Nell in a small voice.

Jesse strangled on a swallow of Bourbon and coughed spasmodically. "Good God in heaven," he said when he got his voice back, "are you out of your— Well, I know prices are up—"

"You haven't been looking, you don't how much up!" said Nell. "I've seen houses half the size on sixty-foot lots for a hundred and thirty. And it really would be a sound investment, Jesse. Really. You just take a look at some of the prices in the real-estate ads."

"Well, I'll go look at it. *Riches profit not in the day of wrath,*" said Jesse. "And at least—I don't need to hear Edgar's advice on that—we could pay it all off at once and not worry about a mortgage. And damn what that stockbroker will say, I'm not fool enough to leave it all in common stock."

Nell heaved a long sigh. "Now that's settled, I'll get dinner."

She had the kitchen cleaned up and the baby settled down, after dinner, when Fran and Clock arrived. Nell started telling them about the house; single-minded, Clock was full of his experience with MacDonald.

"—On a whole acre—"

"—Told you about that body—"

"—Really large rooms, and a lot of old trees—"

"—Suddenly thought, by God, I'd just see what came of it, this MacDonald—"

"—Lovely for Athelstane, he doesn't get enough exercise, if he had another dog to play with, an active little dog—"

"—Just a couple of minutes, Jesse, he just held it and came out with—"

"—But you know he's terrified of Sally, Fran—"

"Listen, calm down and talk one at a time!" said Jesse loudly.

Fran burst out laughing and pulled Clock down to the couch. "You'll have to listen to Andrew's tale first, he's bursting with it. Then we'll find him a new book about ghosts or reincarnation or something and I can hear about the house."

Eventually the girls settled in one corner talking about furniture and drapes and carpets, and Clock told the story all over again to Jesse.

"I never saw anything like it. I don't understand it. How the hell does a thing like that work?"

Jesse regarded him a little sadly. "Just don't fall all the way overboard to complete credulity, friend. Yes, a demonstration like that can be interesting. But even the best psychics aren't a hundred per cent accurate, and they have off days. If anybody knew how it worked we could shut down all the research and start communicating by telepathy. That's what the research is all about."

"Well, I admit I was flabbergasted. I can see that—some of what I've been reading—but it's got to be a special thing, only certain superior people—"

"Oh, no, not even that. Some very good psychics are ordinary people otherwise, not even terribly intelligent. Not always even the high moral principles. But where I part with the earnest researchers," said Jesse, rattling ice cubes in his glass, "is over their trick cards and sensory-deprivation chambers and the computers recording REMs and the fancy Kirlian photography—and even Mr. Backster's polygraphs, him and his emotional dandelions. All the statistical mathematical tables. Trying to pin it down to look at, like a butterfly on a board. When Rhine started all that, forty years back, William Seabrook said, they'll never do it cold, in the laboratory. I don't think so either. It's a thing of the emotions—whatever it is, and whatever else it is. They'll never trap a ghost in a Faraday cage." He laughed. "'Go and catch a falling star—'"

"Faraday cage?" said Clock.

"I'll find you another book."

He couldn't remember how long it had been since he'd found himself on a college campus. Probably one earmark of reaching the thirties was that the college kids looked so damned young. U.S.C. wasn't his alma mater, he didn't know his way around, but a couple of unexpectedly polite, if bearded, students pointed him toward the science building.

Bob Walsh was waiting for him. He looked a little keyed up; he said, "This is great, that you could make it, Mr. Falkenstein: I just hope we get something. Might be absolutely nothing, but Dr. Fredericks says I'm a good subject."

"Did it do it again?" asked Jesse.

"Oh, sure. I was watching it. Five forty-seven, it gave a kind of little whirr—the way a battery clock does, only of course it isn't—and stopped dead." Bob was leading him up some stairs.

"I wonder—" said Jesse.

"Yeah," said Bob thoughtfully. "I do too. If she's around. Knows you—somebody—is looking into it again." They were both silent until they came to a door halfway down the upper hall, and Bob stopped. The door was simply labeled *Humphrey Fredericks*, and Jesse conceived instant respect for a man who omitted adding the initials of all the degrees he probably possessed to his office door.

He was a short, bald, urbane man who shook hands formally. "Bob explained something about this to me, Mr. Falkenstein. I hope we'll have an interesting session."

"So do I." Whatever did or didn't turn up, from this or anything else, it was time he stopped goofing off and got back to work, thought Jesse. He had seen Nell's house this morning, and approved of it. He hoped the old man did too. But it was the hell of a lot of money, and the rest of the money could go as easy as it came.

"As I understand it," said Fredericks, "you want me to take him back to a specific day."

"August 16," and Jesse mentioned the year. "A Friday. A very hot day, and he was at home on Sylvia Drive in West Hollywood. He was eleven years old. We might start the scenario that morning. And, Doctor—"

"Yes?"

"If you can manage it, you might ring me in on it, so he can hear and answer me. I may want to hear some specific answers."

Fredericks pursed his lips. "Don't know. I can always relay, and he's used to working with me."

"However it's easiest."

There was a leather couch in the square little office, at right angles to the desk. Bob took off his shoes and stretched out on it, and Fredericks sat down on a straight chair close beside the couch. He began to talk in a soft voice.

"You will concentrate on the light fixture in the ceiling above you. Keep your eyes on it. Keep looking at it. You are relaxing—all your muscles are relaxing—you have been very tired, but now you are at rest, your whole body relaxing to rest. You are tired and sleepy, now you are going to have a long relaxing rest—and when you wake, you will feel fine and rested. Now you are going to rest—" Fredericks reached around and pushed buttons on the tape recorder on the desk, and it began to purr very lowly.

Jesse had seen it done before, but it was still fascinating. After their long hesitation in accepting it, orthodox science tended to be rather blasé about hypnosis these days, but it was still another mystery of the mind, that thing in man which had nothing to do with a physical brain.

"Now you are asleep. Deeply asleep. You can hear my voice, and you will answer my questions, but you will remain asleep until I tell you to wake. Tell me if you are deeply asleep now."

"I am deeply asleep." The voice was Bob Walsh's, and yet different: a flat emotionless voice. He lay on his back on the couch, flaccid, asleep, and aware. Some inner level was reached and in control.

"Good. You are now going back in time. Back in time. You are now fifteen years old. It is your fifteenth birthday. What are you doing?"

The voice was lighter, more childish. "I didn't want a party. Kid stuff. Just us—Angela's going to be married and he's here—the guy she's engaged to. Dennis—Dennis. He's an all-right guy. Just Mom and Dad—Angela and Dennis—and Monica. We had steak for dinner. Mom and Dad gave me the book on ghost towns I wanted. Angela gave me a lot of tapes, the folk songs I wanted. Monica gave me a new jacket."

"Good. Now you are going farther back in time. Farther back. You will remain deeply asleep, but you will hear my voice and answer me. Now you are all the way back. It is August 16, 197–. You are eleven years old. You are at home on Sylvia Drive in West Hollywood. Can you tell me what you were doing this morning?"

"It's going to be awful hot." The voice was light and thin, more childish yet, much higher in tone than Bob Walsh's pleasant light baritone. "Mom said she'd take Stan and me to the pool this afternoon. We go to the one at the gym club Dad belongs to. She went out to market, and Stan and I just sort of fooled around riding our bikes up and down the block." A pause.

"What else happened?"

"Mike Palfrey and Dave Warren and Larry Foster were playing football in the street, and Stan and I wanted to play but they wouldn't let us. They think they're so great because they're all nearly fourteen—called us little kids, said get lost. They're in junior high. Manuel came in his truck, he cut the Parrs' lawn. Mrs. Werner came out and chased Mike and Dave and Larry away—" He laughed, an explosive little giggle. "That's funny, serve 'em damn well right, they think they're so great on account of being in junior high. Dangerous, she said. Stan and I rode our bikes some more."

"Very well. Now you will move on—" Jesse touched Fredericks' arm and he turned.

"Let him go on from there."

"Very well," said Fredericks smoothly. "You rode your bikes up and down. What time is it now? On that day—a very hot Friday in August."

"It's twelve-thirty."

"What happened next?"

"Mom came home. She fixed lunch for Stan and me. Milkshakes and sandwiches. She said it's too hot to go outside, stay in. Oh, then she was mad! She cussed like anything."

"What was that about?"

"Oh, Dad phoned her. They hadda got out that night—she didn't want to, but there was this new client, he was giving a party and he was going to be worth a lot in commissions and Dad said they hadda go. And Mom cussed and said about her hair, she called up the place and they said two o'clock. She couldn't take us to the pool, she hadda get her hair done. It was a real rotten deal. She said for heaven's sake stay inside, play quiet, it was a hell of a day and she wished she was married to a farmer. But she gave me money for ice cream if the truck came by. And right after she left we saw them again—Mike and Dave and Larry—goin' up the block, they had their bathin' suits, they were going up to get the bus on San Vicente and go to the pool at Fairfax High. That was a real rotten deal too because Mom won't let me go there. Or Stan's mom. Mom says, never know who's hanging around there."

"That's fine. You're doing fine. What time is it now?"

"It's—about—it's two o'clock. The ice cream truck came. It's hot—awful hot. Monica's in the house, she said we were silly, sit outside, but there's nothing to do in the house. I could be reading but Stan doesn't like to read. We ate the ice cream on the front porch. There's a car came up to Mrs. Tredgold's house on the corner and people got out of it and went in. Stan had his new—"

"Describe the people," said Jesse.

"Can you tell me about the people who went into Mrs. Tredgold's house?"

"It was a real ole car, beat up. A girl and a fellow. Stan had his new model airplane but I'm not so interested in that any more. It's only two weeks to when school opens and I nearly said to Stan I'll be glad, but then I didn't, you're not supposed to like school but it's something to do. And Monica said why were we out there in the heat and we went in and had Cokes and then Mom came home. She was still fussing about having to go out. And after a while Stan and I went outside again. It was too hot to do anything."

"All right, that's fine. What time is it now?"

"It's four—four—four-thirty. It's about four-thirty."

"That's right. You're still deeply asleep and relaxed. It is four-thirty in the afternoon of August 16. You and Stan are on the front steps of your house. Can you tell me what is happening now?"

"Nothin'. Nothin'. It's awful hot. Mrs. Werner's out in her front yard. Oh, there's Mike an Dave and Larry, they're coming up the block from the bus. Looks like they hadda great time, they were laughing and fooling around, they went into Mike's house next to the Shellabargers'. I didn't say to Stan but I thought it, must seem funny to come home and nobody there, Mike's mom works all day. There's a red Buick came, it stopped there across the street and I thought it was Mr. Shellabarger, he's got a red Buick just like it, but it didn't turn in their drive. Stopped in front of the house on the corner. Mrs. Tredgold's. A fellow got out and went in."

"What time is it?" asked Jesse quietly.

"What time was that?"

"Uh. It's five after five. It's hot. I wish Stan would go home, I want to go in and read the dog book. Monica says it's silly to read books over but when I like a book I do. I wish Stan would go home but I can't say so. Oh, that maid of Mrs. Tredgold's came out and drove off."

"Is anything else happening anywhere along the street?" asked Jesse.

"Is there anything else happening anywhere around? You can see—you are looking all along the street—is there anyone else there?"

"Uh-huh. There's a man. He just came around from the side street, from Larrabee Street. He's walking up to Mrs. Tredgold's front porch. Seems like he put something in her mailbox. Then he walked down her driveway, away down to the garage. I'm not interested, I'm wishing Stan would go home."

"What's Mrs. Werner doing?" asked Jesse.

"Can you tell me what Mrs. Werner is doing?"

"Uh. She's doin' something in the flower bed by our hedge, she's got her head down right against the hedge. Stan said he hadda be home by six o'clock. I had my watch on, it was twenty-five to six. The guy came out and drove off in the Buick. Monica—"

"What about the man who went down Mrs. Tredgold's drive?" asked Jesse.

"What happened to the man who walked down the drive at Mrs. Tredgold's house? Did you see him again?"

"Uh. No. Didn't notice. Monica—"

"What did he look like?" asked Jesse.

"Can you describe the man who walked down the drive? Try to tell me what he looked like."

"Uh, I didn't— He was just a man. He wasn't very tall. Tan pants and shirt he had on. I didn't see him come back. Stan said he hadda go, he started home on his bike, and I went in. Mom was putting something in the oven. She said to wash, she was still kind of cross, she didn't want to go to that party. Then Dad came home."

"That's fine," said Fredericks. He glanced at Jesse. "You will wake now, and you will feel fine, very refreshed and well. When I count three, you will wake. One—two—three." He snapped off the tape recorder.

Bob Walsh stirred and sat up slowly. He blinked at Fredericks, at Jesse. "Did I—did I say anything interesting, Mr. Falkenstein?"

EIGHT

"I just don't understand how I could have forgotten a thing like that," said Bob. "I told you how Stan and I tried to play detective afterward, think if we'd seen anything supicious— only it was just a couple of days before the police arrested him —Tredgold. But you'd have thought I'd have remembered that, the stranger walking down that driveway."

"You weren't interested at the time," said Jesse. "You didn't take much notice of him, and it slid right down into your sub-conscious mind. Funny all the same. And just who in hell could it have been? Fellow with the throw-away ads— Hell! They're usually casual hired labor, picked up from the dere-licts at an employment agency—or even a Salvation Army mis-sion. They get paid by how many per thousand they distribute, I think. Why did he go down the drive?"

They were standing on the sidewalk in front of the Walsh house, which had been Louise Tredgold's. The rain had held off; the sky was dark and glowering, but it had turned very cold, which in southern California probably meant no rain in sight for the moment.

"You know," Bob said consideringly, looking up the drive, "if I remember what you said about the evidence, the garage door was open and of course the garage was empty. Could it be this guy thought there wasn't anybody home, took a chance to look around the back and see if he could get in?"

"Just on impulse?" said Jesse. "I suppose it could be. But he couldn't get in. The back door was locked, and there wasn't any sign of forced entry. One thing I will say, and mark it well, if you really are going to pass the bar and get to be a practicing attorney. Beware of the positive witness. Mrs. Werner. She was probably honestly convinced that she'd had the block under observation the whole time—but just then, as you now tell us, she was working along a side flower bed and had her back to the street, and she never saw that fellow at all. My guess would be that she was working there the rest of the time until she went in. He could have come back down the drive and gone on down the rest of the block—stuffing ads into mailboxes? One thing I do know, damn it—if that's who he was, it'd be hopeless to get any line on what ad he was distributing, for whom, or who he was." Jesse stared up the straight concrete drive and with little effort he could conjure up that anonymous figure. "It puts a new character on the scene, but whether he had anything to do with the murder—" He lit a cigarette with a snap of his lighter.

After a moment Bob said, "You know, all you told me, the back door being locked and so on— All of a sudden it occurs to me to wonder, did she let somebody in? She could have. Suppose this guy went down and rang the back doorbell, testing whether there was anybody home, and she answered it. That would have been just after Dick Tredgold left. And suppose this character forced his way in, and she ran down to the living room and got hold of the poker to defend herself, and he followed her and got it away from her, hit her to stop her screaming."

Jesse looked at him, struck. "Out of the mouths of babes," he muttered. "That's presupposing this fellow was the casually violent type, maybe hyped up on something—just landing at that particular place that particular time, and having the impulse. Well, God knows there are enough like that walking around loose in any big town. But the house wasn't ransacked —there wasn't anything missing. Barring that diamond brooch."

"I didn't hear about that," said Bob. Jesse told him. "Oh. Well, he could just have snatched that, after he'd killed her, and gone off. If he was one like that, a down-and-out hired to distribute ads, it could be a piece like that would have looked pretty big to him."

"I don't know," said Jesse doubtfully. "I should think he'd have gone on to look for more loot. And of course we're building this out of nothing at all. There's nothing to say—" And then suddenly he let out a loud yelp. "Oh, my God! Oh, my God—but evidence—evidence! Didn't the sheriff's boys even think of that one? My God, Bob, nothing at all tells us that back door was locked *then!* Sure, sure, Jean Clark said it was— but we don't know. All the wild ideas I had—she could have deliberately left it unlocked for the boy friend, and that was why she wanted an alibi at the gas station—and the bungling boy friend arrived too early— But all right. All right, give the lady the benefit of the doubt. Didn't I just say something about positive witnesses? Let's say she just forgot to lock that door, or even forgot whether she had. The sheriff's boys found it locked, Q.E.D., it must have been locked. It may be prejudice, but I do think the L.A.P.D. would have been more thorough. So when our man came down the drive, he found it unlocked, and he slid in to do a little ransacking. And she heard him. Came downstairs and found him, say, in the living room. And if he was the type we've been thinking about, the casual drifter, a wino, a user, it's a type that panics easily. He grabbed up the nearest thing handy, to keep her quiet—he knocked her down, added a couple of blind hits for good measure, and ran. The doctor did say the—mmh—fatal blow was probably accidental. Accidentally fatal, that is. Probably also grabbing that diamond brooch, the only visible piece of loot. I like that very much—it's plausible. Damned plausible. The kind of blind, violent, reasonless crime that happens every day. And if that was at five forty-seven, it doesn't matter a damn whether Mrs. Werner was then facing the street again—he'd go out the way he came, at the back, and through the gate in the wall to the side street."

They looked at each other. Bob was excited. "It hangs together all right—it could have been that way. But is this enough of a reason to open the case again, I mean legally? Showing there was somebody else—"

"No way," said Jesse sadly. "All very thin and iffy. Just a little pointer to what could be the truth. But if that's what happened, Bob, it'd be a million to one anybody could ever track him down now. Find which market, discount house, whatever, was distributing ads by hand that day?—which casual hired hands they paid to scatter the ads about where?"

"Well, I see that," said Bob reluctantly. "I suppose there isn't even any way to try."

"It'd be a miracle if one like that got identified," said Jesse.

They stared at the house, the well-bred-looking house with its square of brick porch confined by the wrought-iron railing, the generous rectangle of green lawn in front with the trimmed hibiscus hedge along one side, the standard tree roses following the curve of the brick walk up from the street.

Manuel appeared in the driveway next door, trundling his rotary lawn mower from the back.

"And you know something," said Jesse. "Between us we've just built that up from not much at all. The man walking down the drive could have been the meter reader, for God's sake. Don't they leave the truck, cover a half block or so on foot?"

"Yeah," said Bob. "But— Well, another thing. What you were telling me about this new—er—friend of hers." Bob was still young enough to feel slightly embarrassed at the notion of anybody over thirty entertaining romantic emotions. "I wonder if he could have had any reason— Oh, I know it sounds far-fetched, but say—well, say she'd found out he was just after her money—or say she'd found out something really criminal about him—"

Manuel had spotted them there, and left the lawn mower and was trudging up to them. "Well, I know it sounds far out," said Bob, "but Mrs. Tredgold was a nice woman—a lady, Mom always said—and if she had found out something—by what you said, she didn't really know much about this character, just taking up with him like that. Suppose she had found out something, and was threatening to tell the police— He could have had a reason to want her out of the way."

Jesse maintained a straight face. "Reaching," he said. "Oh,

I'd like to know something about our Louise's new romance too, but I don't really think it had anything to do with the murder. I don't think. I have been known to be wrong."

Manuel had paused a few feet behind Bob, was waiting to be noticed. Bob discovered him and said, "Hi, Manuel. How's it going?"

"Well. I thought I would tell you, the post office man has left notice of a parcel in the mailbox. He asked me, I told him nobody home. Perhaps you would not find it."

"Oh, thanks very much."

Manuel didn't turn away. "*Pardone,*" he said. "You were talking of the lady who was killed? Of the Mrs. Tredgold?" They looked at him. He was a solid brown man in shabby clothes, with a brown stolid face: perhaps more Indian than Spanish. Among the large Mexican population of Los Angeles, there were all sorts of people, the old-country ones clinging to the language though they might be sixth-generation Californians, the smart new ones picking up American slang, and everything in between. Manuel's English was only slightly accented, but he carried over the more formal Spanish grammar.

"That's right," said Bob, slightly surprised.

"You were saying that she had found a new man," said Manuel. He nodded sagely once. "I had been surprised it did not happen before. She was a very handsome woman. A woman very"—he hesitated and chose—"*agradable.* But you seemed to say that no one knew this man?"

"That's right," said Jesse. "Why?"

Manuel looked thoughtful. "It is a long while ago. There is a man in prison for her death."

"True," said Jesse. "But perhaps all the truth didn't come out at the time. I'm looking into the case again. Do you know anything about this man?"

"Ah?" said Manuel. "One always wondered. Of course they did not ask me questions, because I was not here that day. And—" he looked uneasy—"you will understand, until this moment I did not know that this man was not known to all. The way the lady is so"—he gestured—"at ease of manner, and with me, who only looks after her garden, it is apparent that all is known to the world. But now you say it was not."

"My God," said Bob, "don't tell me you knew about him all the time!"

Manuel looked even more uneasy. "There was no thought of keeping a secret. I did not know he was not known."

"Yes, all right, but how on earth did you know?"

"It was the day before the lady was killed. I was here, working in the garden. In the back. She comes out with the man. She is, as I said, a friendly lady—*muy agradable*. She introduces the man, tells him how I keep the garden in a nice state."

"Don't keep us in suspense," said Jesse gently. "Do you remember his name? What he looked like?"

"Oh yes. I think the lady had been lonely—a good lady, and if she is not young, *pues bien*, it is in age one feels more the loneliness, *¿cómo no?* I thought he would be a good new man for her. A well-looking man, also not young, tall, gray hair, a good face. And yes, I remember the name she said. It was Elting."

"Elting?" repeated Bob doubtfully.

"I am sure. Elting."

"Well, I will be damned!" said Jesse. "Something else right under our noses, if we'd only known where to look."

"I did not know—the thing did not come to my mind until I hear you say—"

"Yes, don't worry about it, Manuel, I'm just glad you remembered now," said Bob fervently. "It's O.K., thanks for telling us."

Looking unconvinced, Manuel trudged back toward his lawn mower. "The way things have been emerging—" said Jesse. "That's very funny indeed."

"Is there any way to find him?"

"It's an odd name—if Manuel's right. Try the phone books, first cast. Though I don't really think—but, hell, we don't know for certain. I'm inclined to like your casual character wandering up the drive, but I don't see any possible way to track him down. The legwork—" Jesse sighed and stepped on his cigarette. "It's tedious enough immediately after the fact, but after eight years—"

Bob drew a long breath. "But when you think what you've found out, just taking a second look—and my character out of my subconscious—well. All I can say is, Mom's going to be furious she missed all this, Mr. Falkenstein. I had a letter from her today, and she didn't like Australia at all."

And the chances were, of course, that the sheriff's boys had walked off with whatever was in the mailbox. Jesse felt morally sure that Clock and his minions wouldn't have overlooked the mailbox—but you never knew. It had looked like an open and shut case.

When Walt Tredgold opened the door and saw him, he said, "I'm beginning to think we should have left bad enough alone. What is it now? Oh, come in."

"Never say die," said Jesse. "On the contrary, we've stumbled on something. A new character on the scene, and it'd be a miracle if we could place him, but I do like to be thorough. Explore every alley, look under every stone. And I wish I could hypnotize you to get at your subconscious."

"For God's sake why?" Tredgold flung himself into a chair. Becky was on the phone somewhere at the back of the house.

"There's just a slim chance you might remember—if, of course, you ever saw it. We can try. The murder was on Friday. The cops had possession of the house to when—remember?"

"Like yesterday," said Walt briefly. "Sunday afternoon. They phoned about one o'clock to say they'd taken the seals off. We were all here. Talking about it. Alida wasn't feeling very well, Becky was trying to get her to lie down. But we all thought about the jewelry at the same time. The house was empty. My God, do you think I could forget any little detail that happened those three days? My God. We were talking about it when that—that cop, that McClure, came with another one and took Dick in for more questioning. Becky couldn't leave Alida, so I—" He stopped. "You want all this? What for?"

"Just go on."

"I went to the house to get all Aunt Lou's jewelry, any other portable valuables. Just what are you after with this?"

"Did you happen to check the mailbox?" asked Jesse.

Walt drew in a long breath and let it out in a gusty sigh. He got out a cigarette and looked at it. "The mailbox," he said flatly. "It's funny, isn't it, how—just when the big important things happen—there's always some little absurd ordinary thing gets associated with it in your mind. Whenever I see a dog scratching fleas, I'm right back there at the Beechams', we were staying with them while Mother and Dad were on that trip, and Mrs. Beecham's telling me how the plane crashed. The mailbox. It's funny you should mention that. I was there at the house, I'd got all the stuff packed in a suitcase and I was at the front door, when I saw a mail truck go by. And I thought I'd check the mailbox. She didn't get much mail, but— I stepped out on the porch and felt inside, there was something there. And just then the phone rang in the hall. I went back to answer it and it was Becky—Dick had just called to say they were arresting him."

"What was in the mailbox, you remember?"

"That's what I meant," said Walt. "It was a little card. For tip-top garden maintenance service call Ernie's Yard Boys."

"Now really," said Jesse to himself, "it can't mean one damned thing, when it comes that easy. . . . A hundred to one it was still there. Damned sloppy cops. A million to one you'd remember it. But damn it, the man was there."

"What man? You mean to say you've turned up something?"

Jesse thought he deserved to hear some of it, and told him. He omitted any mention of the clock, or the new boy friend.

Odd name. He tried the phone books and found just exactly one Elting anywhere in greater L.A. A firm of attorneys in

Beverly Hills: Elting, Rhys, and Danner. No home phone listed for Elting, and the weekend was a lost cause.

There was a listing, astonishingly enough, for Ernie's Yard Boys, All Types of Garden Maintenance and Landscape Design, at an address in Santa Monica. Nell and Fran had taken the baby and gone up to look at the new house. On the chance that Ernie and his boys worked on Sundays, Jesse drove down there, but it was just a small office, a hole in the wall, next to a short-order restaurant and shut up tight.

Well, since he was going to be paying out all that money, he might as well go and take another look at Nell's new love. For something to do, he drove to his office first, circled the block and noted the mileage. Not much further, Nell said blithely; by his reckoning it was another ten miles one way. And on a gray overcast day, with a cold wind moving the clouds rapidly, the tree-shadowed acre nestled away at the end of a winding road looked a little forbidding; the house, with all utilities shut off, was chill and damp. Nell had bullied the keys out of the realtor, saying in twenty-four hours they'd be signing the papers anyway. She and Fran were animatedly discussing future plans for the house, and to Jesse it sounded as if a good deal more money was involved.

"I thought just barely off-white for the living room, because it is rather dark. Drapes with a jungly sort of pattern, bamboo or something, gold and white. The couch needs reupholstering anyway, I thought maybe gold tweed—"

"You want Roman shades for the study," said Fran. "The most practical thing. It's all got to be painted inside. Or what about paneling the study—and the master bedroom? It costs more but it saves money in the long run because you never have to paint. They both get a lot of sun, it wouldn't be too dark. Say a fruitwood shade—"

Athelstane, who had been brought along to visit his new home, began to howl outside, feeling lonely. Fran let him in and he pounced on Jesse delightedly. "There's no point in doing either of the bathrooms over," Nell was saying. "All that tile—real tile—I'm just rather sorry it's green in ours, but it can't be helped. It could be worse. I can have the master bedroom mostly in white—unless we do panel, I could pick up the brown shades and have an avocado carpet. That's another thing. Fran, what about the carpets? We'll have to have all new—"

The baby started to howl and she handed him to Jesse. Jesse looked down at his red-faced protesting offspring and joggled him hopefully. David Andrew gave him a baleful look and went on howling.

On Monday morning they left the baby with Fran and signed all the papers at the realtors' office. The realtor was rather shaken when he discovered that Jesse proposed to pay cash. "A legacy," said Jesse shortly. "No reason to pay interest on that kind of money." The realtor annoyed him by talking about establishing credit; and the stockbroker had already annoyed him by delivering a lecture on the dangers of liquidating assets at this particular economic season. Fortunately he didn't have to listen to either of them.

He dropped Nell off at Fran's and went on down to Beverly Hills.

Elting, Rhys, and Danner looked like prosperous attorneys. Their offices were in a separate and very handsome white brick building with double oak doors. Inside, the carpet felt six inches thick, and there were three smartly groomed secretaries busy inside a three-sided frosted-glass enclosure. One of them came up to him smiling.

"Mr. Danbury?"

"No, sorry. I haven't an appointment, but I'd be obliged if Mr. Elting could spare me a couple of minutes." He gave her a card; she look at it and went away down a hall at the side.

In a minute she came back ahead of a man: a man not tall, but stocky and brisk, a man about thirty-five, with fair hair and a round friendly face. "What can I do for you, Mr. Falkenstein?"

"Nothing," said Jesse. "I'm looking for an Elting who's fairly tall, gray-haired, and about sixty-five."

Elting laughed. "What do you want him for?"

"I think just to talk to. He showed on the verge of an old case I'm looking into, and I'd like very much to know how he got into it. Would you happen to know who he might be?"

Elting looked him over carefully and said, "That could be my uncle. I don't know of any other Eltings around here. He was the original partner—he's retired now."

"Do I look respectable enough that you'll tell me where to find him?"

Elting grinned. "Oh, Uncle Manfred can look after himself. I'll trust you with him. It's six twenty-two Sunny Vista Drive, here."

"Will he be home now?"

"He usually is. What kind of an old case is it, by the way?"

"Murder," said Jesse.

"Oh, that'll please him a hell of a lot," said Elting. "The old boy loves a good crime story. Maybe I'd better tell you how to find the house."

The Eltings were prosperous, all right. It was a big house on, probably, a triple lot: and the house and lots here would be assessed higher taxes than Jesse would be paying on the acre in Coldwater Canyon. It was seventy feet to the front door, and when he got there an honest-to-God manservant let him in, a tall white-jacketed man who left him in a tiled entry hall and bore his card away somewhere. When he came back he escorted Jesse past a cavernous living room to a smaller room down the central hall. A man was sitting at a desk by the window, and turned as Jesse came in.

"Mr. Falkenstein? What can I do for you, sir?" He had been studying a chessboard on the desk before him.

It was, at least, easy to understand why Louise could have been sure this fellow hadn't been after her money. Possibly he had more than she'd had. He was a rather handsome man, with a profile like a Roman coin and fine iron-gray hair. He sat very erect, and he was meticulously clean-shaven and groomed, in a navy suit, immaculate white shirt, and discreet dark tie.

Jesse sat down on the other side of the desk. He was already aware that this part of the story was going to fizzle out to nothing, like every other damned possible lead he had come across. But just to satisfy his curiosity, he'd like to hear about Louise's last abortive romance. "Well, I'll tell you, sir. I've been looking back over an old homicide case. The murder of Mrs. Louise Tredgold. And I've come across several little things that never came out at the time, or during the trial. And I think you could be one of them."

Elting didn't move or change expression for a moment. Then a look of wariness crossed his fine features; slowly he reached up and took off the black-rimmed glasses. "All these years," he said. "That's strange. So—someone knew about us, after all."

"Not really. Nobody knew who you were. But maybe you remember that she did—just once—mention your name to the gardener."

"The gardener," said Elting musingly. "Dear me. I'd quite forgotten that."

Jesse leaned forward. "You don't know a damned thing about the murder, do you? But do you mind telling me what did happen—and what happened to you afterward?"

Elting uttered a little laugh. "It's really a very simple story, Mr. Falkenstein. Do you believe in fate, by the way?"

"No. For better or worse, we're endowed with free will. Karma may be something else again."

"Names for the same things," said Elting. He pinched the bridge of his nose, put on his glasses again. "Well, things happen. Sometimes, it seems, without rhyme or reason. Have you heard how Louise and I met?"

"Yes, at the Chrysler agency."

"That's right. We were both waiting for our cars, and we got to talking. She was a charming woman, you know, very attractive—a nice woman. A very happy person—what is it the youngsters say?—fun to be with. We liked each other. I don't have to tell you that there are times you meet someone, and you—well, click immediately. Know you like each other, you're *simpático*. Oh, it started very simply. We were enjoying our talk, and when the mechanic said my car was ready I suggested we go to lunch together.

"It was just—friendliness—at first, but I think quite soon we both knew that it could grow into something else. Quite soon. But—do you understand?—nothing had been said. For all her surface gaiety, she was really a rather shy woman, and I suppose I've always been reserved. But we both felt something that had been lacking, perhaps—I'd been a widower for six years then, too.

"We'd been out together several times—to dinner, to the theater. We both knew that presently—we weren't rushing it—I would ask her to marry me. She'd told me all about her circumstances, her family. But you can see, just the—the casual way it had come about, no one knew about it at all. I lived alone—my only daughter lives in San Diego, her husband's a navy man. At the time my nephew Donald was practicing in Fresno, we seldom met. I—would suppose that Louise hadn't mentioned it to anyone—wouldn't have until, well, it was definite." He gave Jesse a somewhat bitter smile.

"What I'd deduced. You saw her the day before the murder?"

"Yes. She had asked me to lunch. She showed me over the house, she was explaining how her husband had left it as part of the trust, she couldn't sell it. A daft thing to do—I know I was thinking that it would probably be impossible to rent it, much better for one of the nephews to live in it. When—you understand."

"So what happened? When you heard about the murder—"

Elting said, "Ah, but I didn't. That's what I meant by fate, Mr. Falkenstein. That next afternoon as I was crossing the street, on the way back to my office after lunch, I was struck by a speeding car. In fact, a hit-and-run—the police never found the driver. They didn't expect me to live for quite a while. I was in a coma for three months."

Jesse sat back with a sigh. "So now we know."

"When I finally came out of it," said Elting, "and began to sit up and take notice—everybody was surprised I hadn't suffered any brain damage," and he smiled, "the first newspaper they gave me had a front page story about the result of the trial. A paragraph about the murder, a rehash of the trial. The verdict had been handed in the day before."

"Wonder it didn't send you into shock again."

"I couldn't take it in at once. Louise—gone like that. Then I asked Lisa—my daughter, she'd come up, of course—to get me all the back issues of the *Times*, and I read all about it. Can you understand how I felt, I wonder—or does it seem rather cold-blooded?"

Jesse blew smoke at the ceiling. "She was gone. You didn't know the rest of them. And one of her family had been found guilty of the murder. You wouldn't accomplish anything by injecting yourself into it."

"Hardly." For the first time Elting made a move from the desk. He swung his chair around, and for the first time Jesse was aware that it was a wheel chair. Elting said, "I'm not in this all the while, but the new hip joint they gave me isn't very satisfactory. I have to have a full-time nurse—the invaluable Jenkins, who let you in—and I was forced to retire. I was very tired at that time, Mr. Falkenstein—I was in the hospital for another three months after that—and it just seemed simpler to let the whole thing drop. As you say, she was gone."

"And you've satisfied my curiosity about that," said Jesse. "But, damn it, that gets me no closer to X than any of these other shapeless little bits and pieces I've been dredging up."

"Are you telling me the nephew wasn't guilty? That the case is being— But surely, even if that's so, it would be a waste of time. Eight years. He must be eligible for parole now. It was—"

"Second degree," said Jesse. "Yes, that's just the trouble." He didn't feel especially *simpático* with Elting, but it might help his cerebral processes a little to think back over the case; he gave Elting a capsule report of the evidence, the witnesses, the bits and pieces that had shown up. He didn't mention the clock.

"Oh yes, the medium," said Elting. "I know very little of

such things, but I'm aware that there are some genuine psychics. Louise was convinced that this woman was genuine. I really had little interest in the subject, but Louise was quite a hardheaded woman in some ways, she had helped her husband get his start in business, you know—"

"Yes, and that's another thing," said Jesse. "Why and how was she so convinced? Because the woman's a fraud. She's not even a particularly brilliant fraud—she's a run-of-the-mill con artist with a little rudimentary cleverness at seeming to offer evidence that isn't evidence at all."

"Dear me!" said Elting. "Is that so? It seems odd that Louise was taken in—she told me she'd resisted going to see the woman, she hadn't been interested, but this friend—"

"I had a little thought about it," said Jesse, and told him what it was. Elting gave him one of his wintry smiles.

"There are hazards in all professions. It has always seemed to me, Mr. Falkenstein, that the greatest hazard a lawyer faces is that with time and experience he becomes absolutely cynical regarding the human species."

Jesse grinned. "That's very possible."

"But I don't see what that could have had to do with the murder."

"Damn it," said Jesse, "that Clark woman—if I knew why she'd deliberately told those lies—"

"Legally speaking, if you could ever show the court that they were lies, that would be the best chance to overturn the verdict. There is, of course, very small chance that you could ever do so." Elting bent a sardonic glance on him. "I suppose, Mr. Falkenstein, that there may exist a few human beings able to offer absolutely impartial testimony before a court, completely unswayed by personal opinion or prejudice—but not very many. Not very many."

"Very damned few, in fact," said Jesse.

The little idea in his mind had to do with money. Money always such a nice thing to have. And fate, karma, or blind chance, money didn't always gravitate to the good, the true, and the beautiful.

Sabrina—despite her cunning little play with Maggie Mason —wasn't a great brain. But she had brought Louise enough convincing evidence that she turned into a believer. Louise, not interested at first, not credulous about the spirits. Where had Sabrina got her information?

And it was all very well for Celia Adams to say, Lou never let it make any difference—no, she probably hadn't; it wouldn't have crossed her mind to upstage old friends, just on account of the money. But how had the old friends felt about it?

Regina Moore would have been back at her job today; he hadn't seen her at all. Or Agnes Decker. Poor Regina, always had to work so hard. Could you absolve Celia Adams, silly and shallow, who would be a poor conspirator? It was just a small cynical thought—because, when he thought about it, fifty grand was a considerably larger amount than the Sabrinas of this world generally dealt in.

Celia the link, coming across Sabrina: Regina seeing the possibilities? The flat proposition: we'll feed you the private information to rope her in, and split the take down the middle?

Even if that was so, he didn't see how it could have anything to do with the murder. As late as that last little scene with Dick Tredgold, she had been sold on Sabrina.

But damn it, win, lose, or draw, he would like to know all about this slice of human drama, every element that had gone into making it come out as it had.

She wasn't a big-time operator; she had parlayed superficial cleverness and some dramatic ability into an easy living. That argued of course, a certain cold cynicism, and that was what he played to.

Her private sittings were evidently conducted in the small anteroom off the entry hall of the handsome white building. Steele was there; he recognized Jesse, and his eyes narrowed in brief surprise, but he beamed genially.

"So very pleased to welcome a new patron. If you will come in—my wife is a trifle tired this evening, but we shall hope for a successful session."

She was already seated in an armchair drawn up to a small table, and she gave him a cheerful smile. Her red cheeks and unfashionably done black hair gave her a falsely ordinary, dowdy look. Jesse sat down opposite her and deliberately fanned out ten ten-dollar bills on the table.

"Cards on the table," he said. "You don't need to fake it with me, Mrs. Steele. I couldn't care less how you earn your living. Whatever I know about you and whatever you may tell me, there is no way I can damage your reputation as a psychic. I simply want some confidential information, and very probably it needn't ever go beyond me. Clear?" Steele had ranged himself behind his wife's chair. Neither of them showed any expression at all. "Now," said Jesse, "we all know that the finest psychic in the world has off days when the power doesn't show up. But it's always a pity to disappoint clients, so a little private information is always handy to have.

"I'm talking about Louise Tredgold. It's a long time in the past—it doesn't matter at all now, it's dead and done. And you can't get anything more from her, so that doesn't matter either. I just want five minutes' plain talk from you, Mrs. Steele—I'd just like to know, for my own satisfaction. Who fed you the information you used to convince her?"

"I suppose you know you're talking slander," said Steele. His voice was hard.

"Use some sense. There's no way I can hurt you." Unfortunately. "It's for my own information, and I'm willing to pay for it."

"Get out," said Steele coldly.

"Rodney," she said and her voice cut like a whip. "I'm not used to being insulted, whoever you are. Everybody knows I'm honest—I've got testimonials from people with some big names. You can't come here and insult me."

"Look," said Jesse. "The day of exposing fake mediums is over. Nobody gives a damn." The honest ones, the honest researchers, did; but there really wasn't any point to it any more. "All I want to know—"

"Our dear friend Mrs. Tredgold," she said coldly, "has a very special place in our memories, and I don't care to have my memories spoiled by anyone telling lies about me or her. Louise Tredgold made it possible for us to realize a lifelong dream, to build our spiritual temple, and I'll always be grateful to her dear memory."

"You'd better just go," said Steele. "We have a reputation to maintain."

"My God," said Jesse softly, "she'd already handed it over, had she? And you're really not that good—you had some help." And it wasn't beyond possibility that that operation had led to murder—somehow, some way: money had triggered homicides before.

"I said get out," said Steele.

He felt their eyes on him, to the door. And he felt, for a moment, absurdly angry—the con artist Sabrina getting that money, when the honest seekers after truth were always short of that useful commodity. What the hell did the money matter? The endless laboratory experiments, the staid statistics—it was nothing anyone would ever prove out in a laboratory, or trap in a mathematical table.

Waste of time.

All along the way, he'd been frustrated on this damned thing. For once and for all, and whatever it happened to be, he would like to know the truth. The simple bare truth about what had happened to Louise Tredgold.

It didn't seem that he was going to find out about it soon—or ever.

NINE

On Tuesday morning Clock was sitting at his desk reading a lab report from the arson squad when Petrovsky got back from looking at a new body. "Damn it, it's just a great big question mark," he said, shoving the report over. "You know something? I'm wondering what MacDonald might give us on this thing—I mean, it'd be no harm to go and ask. I mean—"

Petrovsky said, "Oh, now, Andrew—" in a dampening sort of tone.

"We haven't got a smell of this guy, and none of those AWOLs have shown up. I'd just like to hear what he might say," said Clock defiantly. He phoned and talked to Miss Duffy; Mr. MacDonald was there now, and could give him half an hour.

Fired again with the sudden revelation of the possibilities of this thing, Clock dropped his paperwork and presented himself at the offices on Santa Monica Boulevard; he brought along a stack of photographs of the various scenes of arson.

And MacDonald told him nothing at all. His palms flat on the face-down stack of photographs, he merely looked distressed and went into a rigmarole about emotions. "All I get is his fury and frustration—he is so obsessed with destruction!—this is a very confused, destructive mind—he is actually hoping that he will kill someone. It is like a great red maze, this mind, working away, working away on the urge to destroy—"

It meant just damn all. Clock found it mildly interesting as a demonstration; but belatedly he understood what Jesse had tried to tell him. The thing was there all right, whatever it was, but it wasn't anything you could rely on ten times out of ten.

He found himself wondering now if finding that body had been, somehow, just a lucky guess.

———————————

There wasn't any sign on the door of the place, open at such a time. Jesse had landed there at nine o'clock, and sat in the car in front of the place waiting for any signs of life until nine forty-five. He had just concluded that nobody was going to show when a battered Ford pulled up to the curb ahead of him and a wiry young man in tan work clothes got out and walked briskly up to the door, unlocked it and went in. Jesse got out of the car and followed him.

"Excuse me, would you be Ernie?"

"That's me. Ernie Doukmedjian. What can I do you for?" He swung round. It was a tiny office, barely room for a small desk and chair; a door at the rear led to some back premises. "Can't ask you to sit down, we just keep this place for the alley behind, for the trucks. You want to talk about a job? I've got half an hour, have to be at the Angelos'."

From years of habit Jesse handed him a card. "I just want to ask you—"

"Lawyer. Somebody gettin' sued?"

"No. Do you ever distribute advertising cards door to door?"

"Nope," said Ernie. "We really got as much business as we can handle. You tryin' to drum up some advertising?"

"No. Did you ever do that? I've turned up some evidence that ads of yours were being left in mailboxes—by hand—round about eight years back."

Ernie laughed. He was about thirty, lithe and blond and brisk, with a nondescript good-humored face. "God," he said, "I knew the law was slow, thought it moved a little faster than that. Eight years? We was just getting this business started about eight years ago. We did some of that, leaving ads door to door. What's this about?"

"You hire some kind of crew to do that?"

"Mister," said Ernie, "my brother and me and a couple of

friends, we was a bunch of punk kids just outta school tryin' to get started. We didn't have any money to hire anybody—we did that ourselves. I will say, it paid off—brought us some jobs, and the business started to build. Not overnight, but some. You work hard enough, it pays off in the end—we're doin' all right now. Three trucks, and we got over a hundred regular maintenance jobs, that ain't bad, no?"

"No," said Jesse. "So about eight years ago, if somebody found one of your cards in the mailbox, it would have been put there by you or your brother—"

"Or Steve or Sam. What's with all this, anyway?" Ernie glanced at his watch.

"But going door to door, leaving the ads, you wouldn't have any reason to walk down driveways?"

"What the hell is all this?" He was just good-humoredly curious, not belligerent. "This is eight years ago—somebody walking down a driveway? What for, and what's it to you?"

"Well, I'm asking you. You went out trying to drum up business with these ads, then. You and the other three. Why might you have walked down a driveway, at a house where it looked as if nobody was home?"

Ernie shrugged. "This is like Twenty Questions? Well, now I think about it, yeah, I was still learning about the job. You want to build up a good business, you got to give good service. Yeah, a lotta times then, I pass a house and nobody there, I'd take a look at the back, see how it was laid out, get ideas. That was a while back. Hell of a lot of experience under the bridge since then, we know what we're doin' these days. But what the hell's it to you, mister?"

"Damn all," said Jesse disgustedly.

"Well, you know, I'd like to stay and shoot the breeze, it isn't real often we get the nuts in here, but I got to go and mow the Angelos' lawn and prune their roses. I'm real sorry to chase you out," said Ernie.

"Not at all. Thanks very much." Jesse went out and Ernie locked the door after him. A minute later he came out the back, visible because the little office fronted on the lot of a big service station, climbed into a blue pickup truck, and took off. Jesse got back into the Mercedes.

He had never known such a case before, where, every direction he looked, everybody was so helpful, and the answers to questions turned up smoothly—to mean absolutely nothing. The mysteries all getting conveniently explained—to leave a great big blank.

Ernie was the obvious explanation of Bob's subconscious new character on the scene. Jesse had said, a miracle if they could turn him up, and lo, they had, and he turned out—didn't he?—to be a total loss. Meaningless.

But the one deduction out of that little ride on the merry-go-round was that back door: nothing at all said it had been locked when Clark left. Clark could have left it unlocked deliberately or just forgotten it—which she'd never admit, of course.

Round and round on the merry-go-round, and every time it stopped he got a Bronx cheer instead of a brass ring.

And he hadn't seen Regina Moore. He didn't know what good it was going to do, but now he was just doggedly being thorough, going through all the motions.

He stopped at a phone booth, looked up the number, and called Celia Adams. He'd forgotten where the Moore woman worked.

"Oh, she's not working, she's retired, there was quite a good pension and she's got the Social Security—I was just talking to her last night, and we couldn't make out what you were telling me—I mean, after all this time— Oh, I think she'd be home, she doesn't go out much—but, Mr. Falkenstein, I really don't—"

"Thanks very much, Mrs. Adams," he said quickly and hung up. At last, after a couple of days of cold indecision, the weather had made up its mind and in the last ten minutes it had begun to rain again. He sprinted back to the car through an increasing downpour.

He remembered the address: the big old-fashioned apartment building on Romaine Street. It wasn't eleven o'clock when he got there, and the sky so dark it might have been dusk; the rain was a steady drumming on the roof of the car.

Along these old blocks, there were never enough garage spaces for residents, and the cars were left on the street; he found a space half a block up. Like most southern Californian males he seldom wore a hat; he rummaged in the glove compartment, but all the odds and ends in the old Dodge had been tidily cleaned out before it was turned over to the agency, and he didn't even have a newspaper. Swearing, he got out into the rain and sprinted up the block; when he reached the building his trouser legs were dripping.

On the third floor, the bell was answered promptly. "Yes?" she said. The first glance at Regina Moore told Jesse at least one thing: this woman had not been so envious of the money that she'd conceived a scheme for getting some of it. She was a tall thin woman with a long narrow face like a well-bred horse; she had a wide sensitive mouth and tranquil dark eyes, and her short coarse hair was severely cut, dark gray with threads of black in it. She was wearing a tailored navy corduroy dress. He opened his mouth to introduce himself and she said, "Now let me guess. Celia gave me quite a graphic description, but I won't repeat it. Would it be Mr. Falkenstein?"

"That's right."

"Well, come in. I'm afraid I couldn't make out from what Celia said, what it's all about. She seemed to think Lou's murder was gong to be tried all over again. What is it all about?"

She was an eminently intelligent woman, the dark eyes shrewd. She asked him to sit down, told him it was too early for her to offer him a drink, and waited for him to say something. "That might be looking ahead," said Jesse. "Reopening the case again—I don't know. I keep running into dead ends."

"You don't mean you are investigating all over again. Why?"

He told her a little about it. She sat smoking quietly, listening with a little frown.

"That seems rather incredible," she said. "And yet—I didn't really know them. The Tredgolds. Oh, I'd met them on and off for years—not often. Lou always had an open house party at Christmas. But years ago, the boys running in and out—just boys, and I don't know much about children. And then they were in college, and her husband died, and both the boys married. You couldn't say I knew them—as people. And of course it was just as incredible at the time—one of them killing her."

"You didn't doubt it then?"

She threw out a brusque hand. "Why? The police usually know what they're doing. Certainly, I had every sympathy for the supposed motive—not to be flippant about it," and she laughed. "Lou was really being very tiresome over that silly medium. She seemed to have lost all her common sense." She tapped a new cigarette on the coffee table. This was a typical apartment of its vintage, rather nondescript shabby furniture, an ancient oriental rug here, glimpse into a dinette, a bedroom at the opposite side of the living room; but there was a comforting permeation of plentiful gas-furnace heat, and there were books everywhere. Shelves in here and beyond the door to the bedroom, with the marching rows of books nearly to the ceiling. She had been sitting in the armchair where she sat now, reading; the book open and face down on the ottoman was an old John Dickson Carr, *The Problem of the Wire Cage*.

"She'd talked to you about it?"

"Oh, I wouldn't listen to her. It was all so foolish—but I was surprised at Lou. She usually had more sense than that, if she wasn't exactly an intellectual." Suddenly she laughed. "I can see you're wondering how on earth we ever got together—Lou and me and Celia Adams and Agnes—"

"I haven't met Mrs. Decker."

"No? She's rather like Celia—all wrapped up in her grandchildren these days." She lit the cigarette and sighed on a long exhalation of smoke. "Time, Mr. Falkenstein. It's an awful thing. You're bosom buddies with a few girls at school, and the next thing you know you've all grown in different directions, you aren't the same people at all really, but of course you've known each other forever, you know each other so well, you still think of each other as old, close friends. As a thousand other people have said, life is a funny proposition." She smoked in silence for a moment. "It wasn't very often I went

out with them—the way we were going to that night. I'm a
solitary, and after all the years of an eight-to-five job I'm very
happy to stay home—then, of course, I was still working and it
usually took dynamite to get me out at night. I'm always perfectly happy to stay at home with a book. But I knew I should
get out once in a while, not grow into a hermit. Lou and Celia,
of course, there was nothing they liked better than getting all
dressed up to go out somewhere—" She chuckled. "Lou did
enjoy having the money, and goodness knows they worked for
it and deserved it. What did you want to ask me, by the way?"

"I couldn't say," said Jesse. He'd really come to see her to
round it off in his mind; now she'd described Agnes to him,
there wasn't anyone else in the case even to go to look at.

"Do you really think he was innocent of the murder?"

"A lot of things say so. Not much chance of proving it now,
or spotting the real X. I think so, yes. Set of circumstances put
him in a little trap. And that Clark woman—at the trial—"

"I was there, of course. I thought she seemed—vindictive.
Which was odd, because Lou was always very nice to anyone
who worked for her. What little things say he's not guilty?"

"Traffic in Hollywood for one," said Jesse, and told her about
that. "He couldn't possibly have left Sylvia Drive later than
five thirty-five and made it home by ten past six. He was lucky
to do it in that time."

"But didn't the police—"

"Oh, he could have made it quicker. Just. It wouldn't have
taken long to kill her. And it looked like such an open and shut
case."

"But what can you or anybody possibly do about it now? I
may be just a cold-blooded practical female, Mr. Falkenstein,
but as far as I can see Dick Tredgold is acting like an idiot.
The only way he'll leave prison is if the real killer is found—
honestly! Honestly! When he could walk out tomorrow and
pick up the threads of his life—money and a job waiting."

"Matter of principle. Women never understand principles,"
said Jesse.

"Oh, don't we? And maybe we've got all the more common

sense for that. He's not a fool—he should be able to see for himself that if neither the police nor those private detectives could turn up any more clues at the time, a fat chance anybody would have now. The man's an idiot," said Regina Moore.

"He's been reading metaphysics."

"You think that explains it? Of course I suppose he's got plenty of time to sit and brood, they don't work them a twelve-hour day any more, do they? And what in heaven's name led him to metaphysics? The little I knew of Lou's nephews, they were firmly brought up to be all solid shrewd business. I can't make the man out. You really think he didn't do it?"

"Well, there's something else that I—um—rather like," said Jesse, and told her about the clock.

"Now that," she said thoughtfully, "is very interesting."

"You don't like mediums."

"My dear man," she said impatiently, "I can be allergic to probably bogus mediums without being a complete disbeliever in all the funny things that happen in this world. That's one of the commonest funny things, isn't it—the clock stopping when somebody dies."

"It is. The point is, if she died at five forty-seven, he couldn't possibly have done it."

"No. I'll tell you something. If it means anything at all," said Regina Moore seriously, "that clock belonged in Lou's family. Her great-grandfather brought it with him when he emigrated from Germany. His name was Bergner. That was in 1857. It went to Lou's mother when he died, and when she died it came to Lou. I remember that clock, as long as I knew Lou. If it's the same one—an oak wall clock with a pendulum."

"That's it. That says a little more, maybe."

"It's funny. But when I can see all this, surely an honest-to-goodness lawyer ought to see it even clearer—the whole silly idea is a waste of time, and if you want to know, I think you're as big an idiot as Dick Tredgold for spending any time on it at all."

"And I think I'm beginning to agree with you," said Jesse.

"I'd better go back to the office and tell the girls to start making appointments again." He got up.

"Trust a couple of high-principled men to make fools of themselves," she said, but there was a smile in her dark eyes. At the door she said, "Besides, does it matter now, as far as Lou is concerned?"

"Don't you think it does?" said Jesse. "Don't you think it matters—to her?"

"I don't know," she said, looking troubled. "How can we know?"

But, he thought, driving slowly through the blinding sheets of rain, the day so dark that headlights shone fuzzily through the mist, but—! If Bob's new character on the scene was now neatly explained away—and it was a miracle in itself that Walt had remembered that little inconsequential thing—he was thinking now that the likeliest answer was something very like what they had postulated. The drifter, the derelict, wandering by chance along there— That quiet upper-class neighborhood? Well, it wasn't that far from a couple of freeway exits, and that kind often got around by hitchhiking now. A young one, that idea said: one of the roaming younger generation, and so many of those intermittently or perennially on the grass, the speed, the uppers and downers.

—Wandering up that block, on Larrabee Street (and damn whether Mrs. Werner was watching Sylvia Drive or not). The wall around the Tredgold yard was augmented by shrubbery, but over the side gate you could see the door to the garage; it had been up and the garage empty. So, he would have thought nobody was home, the possible casual loot to be picked up.

It made the time even tighter. Almost like a French farce with bedroom doors opening and shutting. Dick driving off at just five thirty-five. Almost at once Ernie, or one of those four, passing by, going down that drive, probably for a quick glance into the back yard. Five thirty-seven to eight? The derelict type would have had his hand on the side gate then. Ernie going off, completely unnoticed by Mrs. Werner. And so the back door must have been unlocked; the derelict type discovers it and goes in. Say about five-forty. Meanwhile, Louise had gone back upstairs to finish dressing—to put on her jewelry, *vide* Becky. She had the diamond brooch in her hand when she heard something downstairs—and then—

Well, she may have thought it was Clark come back for something, or Dick. At any rate, she didn't call out—she just came down to see. And surprised the derelict type in the living room. And he, possibly high on something, trapped with her at the door, he grabbed up the poker—

Jesse sat waiting for the light at Third and Western and thought sadly, Just the way it might have happened: and there was about as much chance of proving it as of setting the earth revolving the other way round.

—It wasn't just quite so likely, but it could have happened, the derelict as he fled the way he'd come automatically shoving in the button in the back-door knob so it locked after him. It was a fact that fingerprints often didn't show up where they should have. He could have done that.

No chance at all. No chance of ever getting any smell of any idea who the derelict had been. Where from. Where he went. As he'd said to Bob, it was exactly the shapeless, reasonless kind of crime that happened too often in any big city. An hour after a thing like that happened, the cops too often hadn't a single lead as to where to look. Eight years later—

He got around onto Wilshire at last, and had to drive even slower; this was a downpour such as southern California once in a while did get, reminding natives that it was, after all, desert country given to the extremes. Absently he blessed his guardian angels who had arranged that his permanent parking slot was in the underground garage of the building. He took the elevator up to the third floor, thinking that he'd have a sandwich sent up from the drugstore.

"Well, good afternoon," said Jean and Jimmy in unison.

"Don't be cross, girls." He took off his wet raincoat and hung it up. "I think I've recovered from my momentary aberration. You can start taking appointments again. And you can go to lunch together now."

"In this flood?" said Jean. "Thank you, no. We'll have something sent up. I'm just keeping my fingers crossed that the car roof is tight."

There was a coffee maker in their little private cubicle; a very sodden-looking boy presently brought up sandwiches in wet paper bags. Against his will Jesse was staring at the rain streaming down the window and thinking about the derelict when Jean brought him a telegram. He opened it absently.

It was from the private eye in Chicago. It contained an address and telephone number for Moira Cheney of Oak Park.

Jesse looked at it and sighed. To the bitter end, he thought. He looked at the clock; it was twenty of two. Twenty of five in Chicago: as good a time as any to call.

He dialed direct, and after three rings a pleasant female voice answered. "Mrs. Moira Cheney?"

"Why, yes."

He gave her the quickest, easiest explanation: a book about the case, he was working with the co-operation of the family. He understood she had been an old friend of Louise's, that they had corresponded since she had moved east.

She said doubtfully, "Yes, that's right. But—just what do you want of me?"

Jesse didn't know himself. "When was the last time you heard from Mrs. Tredgold, before she was killed? Do you happen to remember?"

"Why, yes," she said. "Yes, I do. That's really rather strange, you calling just now and asking that. I was just thinking about it the other day. I was going through some things—I'd kept it because—well, I suppose it was just sentiment. My first husband and I—and Lou and Walt—we were young couples together, you see what I mean. I'd known Lou so long. There wasn't anything in it, but I kept it."

"Kept what, Mrs. Cheney?"

"The last letter I had from her. She wrote it that very day—the day she was killed—that terrible way. She—"

Jesse's hand tightened on the phone. "August 16?" he said. "But how would it have got mailed? When did you—"

"Oh, she didn't write many letters, she'd just have left it for the mailman, in fact she said—"

"You've still got it? Could you get it and read it to me—if it's not private—please?"

"Why, surely—" She sounded a little bewildered. "There's nothing in it really." He waited, and she came back and began to read him banalities. Lou had had another private sitting with the wonderful psychic, and Walter had given her such a loving message. She had a devastatingly becoming new hat. She was planning a baby shower for Alida, such a dear girl. Both her boys had turned out so well, such good boys, Walter was proud of them, she knew. And then— "'I had a frightful scene with Mrs. Clark a little while ago, and I've fired her. After all these years! But the last few years she's got ruder and ruder, and this piece of insolence was just the last straw. I'm sure I can find someone nicer to have around who can do the work as well. I must fly, it's after three and time for the mailman, so I'll just say 'by for now, more later, love, Lou.'"

"Angels and ministers of grace!" said Jesse.

"What did you say?"

"That's it? Mrs. Cheney, thanks so very much. I may want a copy of that letter—if so I'll get back to you." He put the phone down. "I will be damned," he said to himself. "I will be— Was it as little a thing as that? Could it have been? But—"

He looked at the clock. It was two-twenty. Rest homes, he thought, operated on hospital hours; the shift would change at three o'clock. He took up the phone again, and got through, was put on hold, and fumed for three minutes until Walt Tredgold's heavy voice came on the line.

"Listen," he said rapidly, "I'm sorry not to give you more notice, but this came up all of a sudden. I've got a line on Clark, something that could explain those lies, and I'm going to tackle her, but I think I'd like a witness."

"Tell me when to come," said Tredgold, "and where."

Jesse gave him the address on 112th. "It's a hell of a way, I'm sorry. I think she gets off at three, she might be home by three-thirty."

"I'll be there."

Just in case this turned out to be a real break in the case, Jesse unhooked the tape recorder, slid batteries into it, and a new sixty-minute tape, put it in his breast pocket. He looked at the windows; the downpour had let up very slightly.

But it was a tedious drive all the way down there, and slow going on streets that were partially flooded, some intersections a foot deep in dirty water. The rain was still heavy enough that the headlights only blurred the dimness. He found a slot for the Mercedes and beat his way back to the building with lowered head, coat collar turned up. Inside, the roar of the rain was hardly muted by the jerry-built walls.

Up there in the narrow hall Walt Tredgold was waiting for him. He was less wet than Jesse in a handsome English raincoat, carrying a wide-brimmed hat. "She's not here yet, at least not answering the door. I suppose I shouldn't have tried—but I got here five minutes ago, and you said—this damned woman—"

"Damnation," said Jesse. "But it's a quarter of four, she might have stopped somewhere on the way. This came out of the blue," and he told him about Moira Cheney.

Tredgold looked incredulous. "But that couldn't have been the reason—just that? I can't believe—and it's queer Aunt Lou didn't—"

"Tell your brother. I think she would have, but if you remember he annoyed her by some joking reference to the tame medium, and she got off on that. I don't know, but—"

The door to the elevator, around the corner of the cross hall, clanged; they both fell silent. Jean Clark came around the corner and up the hall. She was limping slightly. She carried a plastic shopping bag as well as a shabby black handbag; she looked very wet and tired. As she came closer she glanced up and saw them and stopped.

"We'd like to talk to you, Mrs. Clark," said Jesse.

"Well, I don't want to talk to you," she said.

"Nevertheless, you're going to," said Tredgold harshly. "Now. Inside. Open the door."

"You can't give me orders any more." But she found the key in her handbag, opened the door. "I suppose you'd just force your way in," she said sullenly. Jesse closed the door behind them. It was a bare box of a place: a tiny living room with an old day bed, one armchair, a straight chair, a black and white TV in one corner. Through one narrow door there was a smaller bedroom with a single bed; through another, a slot of a kitchenette. She dumped the shopping bag on the day bed and her handbag beside it. "What do you want?"

"We've just found out," said Jesse, "that the day she was murdered, Mrs. Tredgold had fired you from your job there. Why?"

"Oh, you've just found that out," she said. "And you wonder why. All right, I'll tell you why—*Mister* Walter Tredgold," and she took one step toward him almost as if preparing physical attack. Her mouth drew back in a vicious little smile. "I'll tell you! You going around in your fine clothes, in your fine cars, your wife all tarted up in her fur coat—and Mrs. Louise Tredgold with all her diamonds—all of you with all that money —*that I should have had half of!* All these years, making do at the dirty jobs, cleaning up after other people, and I ought to be thankful for steady work! Oh, I'll tell you all about it, Mr. Walter Tredgold—and all about your fine charitable uncle! I can tell you!"

She was talking directly to him, ignoring Jesse: her eyes were bright and hard as little diamonds themselves. "Your fine hard-working self-made uncle, Mr. Walter Tredgold. I don't suppose you ever heard the name of Alfred Hoskins, did you? Oh no, you wouldn't—well, he was the man who should've been your uncle's partner, and he'd have ended up with just as much money as you if he had been. They'd talked about it, you know—I'd heard them. Alfred Hoskins was my dad, and he was the first man your uncle ever hired, to run that second grocery he opened up. And it wasn't going so good, and money was tight, and it looked like they'd have to close, take a big loss. Oh, I heard 'em talking about it—your uncle, he came to see Dad in the evening, talk money. They didn't know I listened at the door—I was only a kid, thirteen, fourteen, but I could add two and two. Dad said they could get the insurance—he knew a way to make a fire look like it happened from bad wiring— and at first, your uncle, oh no, he couldn't do that. But he come to see it was the only way, get the insurance and they'd be safe —Dad was going to do it and then they'd be partners—"

"That's a damned lie!" said Tredgold.

"Oh no, it's not, Mr. Walter Tredgold—I was there! Only your fine honest uncle, at the last minute he tried to back out, got cold feet. Called on the phone—Dad was in the garage getting the stuff ready—and said I was to get him, tell him not to go ahead with what they planned—I told him Dad had already left. If they didn't do it there wouldn't be a job or money for groceries—didn't I know? I had to learn to manage, Ma dying when I was ten. So Dad did it, and nobody suspected, your uncle got the insurance—"

"*Oh, my God,*" said Tredgold.

"—and didn't he have the damned gall, back out of the whole deal, his conscience get to bothering him!—Dad persuaded him against his will! Oh, sure, he paid Dad—a measly five thousand, and how long did that last? His old job back! And after that, he's making money hand over fist, more and more and more. And when Dad got on the drink and lost his job, your fine uncle Walter Tredgold prob'ly never knew about it—some general manager did the firing— All that money we should've had! Oh, I told Dad he ought to go see him, he could tell the tale on Mr. Walter Tredgold—we were due some of that money! But he was scared to do that, he never would. You better believe I wasn't scared, I can tell you that. Time that no-good bum I married walked out and left me broke with two kids, I had enough of living cheap—I went to Mr. Walter Tredgold and I told him what I knew. I sure did. And he was one with a head on him, Mr. Walter Tredgold was. Wasn't he nice and kind and generous! Told me I'd just got the wrong idea about that time, they'd just talked business, and of course I hadn't any proof at all any such thing ever happened—but he surely wanted to look after the daughter of an old employee—Oh, sure! Gave me a good job doing his wife's housework—but all the time I was there he slipped me double pay every week, and I knew what it was for and he knew what it was for."

"Jesus," said Tredgold numbly. "No, I don't—"

"He told me once he'd see I got something in his will, but he never. He couldn't 've expected to die like that, he wasn't really old. But that was the end of it—because your dear sweet little aunt Lou, she never knew about it—about the fire. And I'm not that big a fool, try to tell her, she'd never believe me. Paying me two bucks an hour, clean the floors and wash her windows, and I see her spending money like water—clothes and jewelry and a new car and dinner out at fancy restaurants and going to the theater—I should've had some of that money—none of you'd ever have had any money, Dad hadn't set that fire way back then! Her, giving me her secondhand clothes—so kind and generous!

"Oh, but I had a laugh on her! I thought I did!—and even that went all wrong. Her telling me about that woman pretended to talk to dead people—I know about *them,* they got ways find out things and get people believing it's dead people come back. It was the very next day I was at the Shellabargers', this woman come to the door, said she was come about insurance or something, ask about Mrs. Tredgold, and right off I cottoned who she was, and I told her so. I said I'd tell her whatever I knew, so she could fool Mrs. Tredgold good —I wanted to see that! Couldn't I tell her things! Working there all that time—and I always snooped into things, I like finding out things. That's how I knew about Dick taking off with that girl, snooping on your aunt and uncle talking private about it. I told her a lot of stuff, and she paid me a hundred bucks. She could see I liked doing it, wasn't ever going to tell on her. So she could make your aunt believe she was hearing from dead people. Oh, that woman had her fooled good—I liked hearing about that.

"But then that day—that day—hotter than the hinges of hell it was, and all the windows to wash—she said wait till it cooled off, but I knew she didn't care, and everybody always said I was a good worker, I do a job when it oughta be done— Amy and her boy friend come, asked me for the loan of five bucks—I only had ten on me—and just after, she come into the kitchen and started telling me all about this woman again—and just like—" her voice rose in fury—"just like she says she's gonna buy a new hat, she tells me she's given that woman *all that money*—fifty thousand, *fifty thousand*—money should've belonged to *me!*—so she could start a church of some kind—*all that money*— And it was like something busted right inside me, I started telling her—*my money*—the fire Dad set and the way we got treated— She wouldn't believe me, she wouldn't listen, she just got awful mad, she got her purse and paid me and said I should finish out the day and never come back—and she went upstairs—

"And I never got to tell her how I helped *that woman* fool her—that made me madder than anything else—by the time I thought about it she was in the bathroom, getting ready for her fancy party—oh, if I could just have told her— But it wasn't no use. I saw that then. She wouldn't believe that either, no use trying to tell her." She stopped talking suddenly, and she was panting a little.

"Oh, for Christ's sake—" Tredgold was looking white and shaken.

"So that," said Jesse, "was what you had against the family. Why you told those lies in court."

And she stabbed out at him like a snake striking. "Nobody can say I told any lies in that court! I told the truth the way I remembered it, and nobody can ever prove different!"

Jesse had completely forgotten to switch on the tape recorder. Tredgold turned and wrestled blindly with the door, stumbled out to the hall. The last look Jesse had at her, she was standing there breathing hard, her eyes bright with hate.

He shut the door behind him. "Are you all right?"

"No," said Tredgold thickly. "My God. My God. If that's true—have to repay that insurance. Have to—" He took a breath and straightened. "And we thought—we thought something, maybe, to show she had told those lies—to show Dick was telling the truth. But—that's—nothing—to do—with—the murder."

"No," said Jesse. "It's nothing at all to do with the murder."

TEN

"As far as the murder is concerned," said Nell, "all I can say is—"

"Well?" said Jesse as she hesitated. Fran was curled up on a corner of the couch, and Clock had wandered into the study looking for a book.

"I'm afraid I'll have to agree with Regina Moore. The whole idea was just ridiculous—it'd be impossible to find out about it now."

"In fact, a very impractical proposition," said Fran. "Yes. It seems to me that Dick Tredgold ought to be smart enough to take the cash and let the credit go, and don't say anything to me about principles."

Clock came back into the living room carrying a battered copy of *Raymond* in one hand and *Between Two Worlds* in the other. "That murder," he said. "Whoever did it, it was a two-bit affair like any that happens in any big town five times a week. Somebody grabbing up the blunt instrument on impulse. I think you read it right, the drifter just happening by. But you'll never get your boy off the hook legally, and at this late date what's the odds? It doesn't really matter."

"I wonder if I should let you have that," said Jesse, looking at *Raymond*. "The truth always matters, Andrew."

"I think I might have looked closer at the driving times," Clock said, "but I'm not going to say I wouldn't have dropped on him too, if it had been my baby. He looked so obvious, and most homicides are anything but complicated."

"How right you are," said Jesse. "I think you'd have spotted the card in the mailbox too, but that's very much a side issue. If I wanted to try, I could show by implication that Clark's testimony was suspect, but this much later, with him already eligible for parole, no court would even schedule a hearing—no point."

"You'll just have to persuade him to take parole," said Fran. "Nobody'll ever know who killed her now."

Jesse stood looking into the crackling little fire on the hearth, his back to them. "Well, that's not quite right," he said. "Two people know. The murderer. And Louise Tredgold."

———————

Walt Tredgold looked at him as if he'd suddenly grown horns and tail. "I refuse to be associated with such an outlandish notion," he said.

"My only thought was, it might help the contact if you were present," said Jesse.

"I took you for a sensible man," said Tredgold stiffly.

"Well, I believe in solid evidence," said Jesse patiently. "Tell me, Mr. Tredgold, do you believe we get annihilated when we die—everything we are and know, all experience and emotion just blown into dust?"

"I—well, no, of course not. I'm afraid I've never been a churchgoing man—"

"It hasn't got anything to do with churches or sects. Then, you know, you've got to accept that she's somewhere—over the line, still pretty much the same person she was here. With the same interests and concerns. Don't you think she'd still be concerned for you and your brother—just as she always was?"

"Yes," said Becky Tredgold. She had been listening in silence; now she said again suddenly, "Yes, she would be. Don't be stuffy and stupid, Walt. I've read enough to know that it isn't all imagination and fraud. I'd be interested, Mr. Falkenstein—but I have to live with this man, and I don't suppose you'd ever convince him."

"Don't you think she'd have cared about what happened?" said Jesse to Tredgold.

"I don't think anybody can know about these things," said

Tredgold. "I'm a practical man, not a godforsaken visionary. Oh, for God's sake. I'll just have to write Dick, try to talk sense into him." He looked at Jesse with cold astonishment, with something like disgusted wonder.

"Well, of course," said DeWitt, "there's nothing at all unusual about that. What else are practicing mediums doing all the time but contacting specific individuals? But you know as well as I do, there are so damned many variables." He took off his glasses and began to polish them carefully on his handkerchief. "We don't know much about how it works, but there are evidently difficulties in making contact—different levels of vibration, wave lengths—we just don't know enough. And it varies so widely with individuals—harder for some to get through than others. Apparently no one's ever tried to contact her—the very idea may be so strange to her over there that she wouldn't accept it, or try. True, by what we know, others there try to help—provide energy, advice, whatever. But it can be a chancy thing. On—er—both sides. Even if she was anxious to get through, she might not be able."

"We can have a try. That clock—"

"Oh, now, you've read the pertinent literature. The clock," said DeWitt, "like all the other clocks doing queer things, is unlikely to owe its antics to any individual personality. More likely some purely mechanical effect, psychokinesis—which we really know nothing about yet."

"Yes," said Jesse. "Another thing. Time doesn't seem to mean much over there, which may be a factor in our favor. But something else too—I don't feel that Louise was such a lofty spiritual character that she drifted away to any upper realms. She liked life here, she enjoyed the money and all the nice physical things, all the things on this level—I have a hunch she wouldn't be far away. And probably very much concerned with what was going on, with the people she loved. For all we know, William, she's tried to get through to anyone she could reach, only nobody heard her or understood what she was trying to say."

DeWitt laughed. "Possible. Enough garbled messages always come through."

"Damn it," said Jesse, "I'd like to try—see what we might get."

———————————

"You," said Dick Tredgold, "are about the queerest lawyer I've ever run across. Not that I've had much to do with lawyers. Before I met Featherstone, that is. The company attorneys lurk in leather-padded offices, poring over the fine print. And I can just imagine what Walt said to you—or can I?" There was a quizzical smile in his eyes on Jesse.

It had been an exhilarating drive up the coast that early morning, the rain blown away by a strong west wind, the air sparkling wine-cold, and fat white clouds like spring lambs scudding across the sky. The tight rows of drab white cottages, the big central building, were in sober contrast. Jesse regarded Dick Tredgold with mild irritation, perched on the straight chair with the meshed grille between them.

"Probably," he said, "You and your metaphysics. I just want to be sure you understand the possibilities here. And the other way round."

"Oh yes," said Dick. "Though I doubt very much that a ghost would bring you anything acceptable to a court of law."

"And even that has happened," said Jesse. "She loved you, she'd care what happened to you."

"Yes, she would have," agreed Dick soberly. Then he added with a crooked smile, "I had a most persuasive letter from Walt—he must have been reading Dale Carnegie. I don't think he's got any remote inkling of what prison's done for me. If I decide to take that parole, I'm afraid Walt and I won't be seeing quite eye to eye the way we always did. You could say that the experience has widened my horizons, as it were."

"Yes?" said Jesse. "Well, you'll have to sort that out with him if the time comes."

"Oh, I haven't decided to take it yet."

"I just hope you realize the possibilities," said Jesse. "You could make the difference between getting something or nothing. You're the focal point—the vital link, it could be—for her, between there and here. It might be very damned important that you try to co-operate."

"All right," said Dick. "I accept that. I—" He bit his lip and looked at the floor, "It always bothered me that we were angry with each other when she died. I'll try to help—however I can."

"What's your routine here? Are you free and alone at 8 P.M.?"

"Absolutely. Until ten, lights out."

"Yes. Well, at 8 P.M. every night this next week, will you just sit quiet, think about her—go over old memories of her—try to reach her and help her make contact. Hold the positive thoughts. I know it doesn't sound like much, but very little things can sometimes make a difference."

"I'll try. I don't know what you think you might get," said Dick curiously. "The concentrated effort, to get the usual banal anonymous ditherings—I am well and happy and send my love to all?"

"On occasion," said Jesse, "more concrete communications have got across. Why the hell d'you think I drove all the way up here to see you?"

"All right—sorry. I'll try to believe that. I'll try to help."

"You can concentrate too much power, you know," said De-Witt.

"Let's start out with the full battery," said Jesse, "and see what happens."

DeWitt always had feelers out for any possibly promising, developing mediums, and was working with several young ones. But on his permanent staff, so far, were only the two trance mediums, Wanda Moreno and Cora Delaney, besides the psychometrist MacDonald. MacDonald had said they didn't want him and Jesse said oh yes, they did. Wanda was the younger, in her late twenties, a rather plain blonde; only under DeWitt's urbane tutelage had she stopped being afraid of her abilities and begun to use them constructively. Cora Delaney was a plump comfortable brunette in her forties, who had worked for some years with the Parapsychology Institute in New York. Both of them fortunately possessed husbands who were sympathetic to what they were doing.

They sat the first evening in the little study of the offices on Santa Monica Boulevard. Jesse had got Becky Tredgold to give him Louise Tredgold's wedding ring and the other ring she had habitually worn, and he handed them to MacDonald sitting on the couch. The two mediums were in armchairs across the room.

"Oh," said MacDonald at once, "she was overshadowed by a much stronger character most of her life. A rather materialistic man. Tea. A large cup of tea? Tea and coffee, tea and coffee, and there's a large sign—tea."

"Yes, that's all very well," said Jesse. "We know all that."

MacDonald fingered the rings in silence, and DeWitt opened the session. "We are trying to make contact with Louise Tredgold. If there is anyone who can help her come to us, we ask that help. Louise Tredgold. Someone she loves is also trying to help. Has she anything to say to him—to us?" There was a long silence. They had left the lamp on in the corner, and there was a pleasant low light in the room. "She knows that an injustice has been done—we are trying to find the truth. If Louise can help us find the truth, we ask her to try. Anyone who can help her, please try."

After a while Wanda said, "It's all dead, Mr. DeWitt. I can feel it. There are too many of us here."

"A negative charge," said MacDonald the electrician. "Try lightening the load, Mr. Falkenstein."

He and Wanda went into the next room and DeWitt changed the lamp to the lowest of its three-way positions. They sat in silence for a while, until Cora Delaney began to talk in a low voice.

"There's somebody. Somebody helping, because she does so want to come, but it's hard. They told her she could, she'd have to try very hard, not easy. What you want to say, it slides off into something else because you feel things and the feelings get through instead. Feelings. There is someone helping her. Louise, Louise."

"That's right," said DeWitt in his normal voice. "She's just to take her time, we're here waiting, there's no hurry."

"Louise, Louise. I want to tell you because I know what it is you want. Tried before, tried tried tried to tell because all wrong. I was so surprised to find myself here. She is saying, now she's losing contact—I must try, because of the boys."

"Yes," said Jesse quietly. "We know she's concerned for the boys. We want to help her about that."

The medium was silent and then: "Someone told her she could make contact and she tried. But it wasn't enough. They tried to help, but she's gone."

After another half hour they agreed that was all they'd get in that session.

They tried with Wanda the next night, but she got nothing relevant at all; contact had been made, however brief, with Cora, so they started over again with her.

"We are waiting for Louise. Please help her to come again through this instrument—she knows it is important, there is something important she has to tell us. We are waiting."

As usual, the medium began describing an inner vision, sliding occasionally across to the first person as the intensive emotion of the other entity took over. "She was surprised to find what had happened. It didn't seem important and then it was important. But the boys—the boys—she would have been perfectly happy but there was something wrong, something she had to tell someone— Oh, I want to tell you something. I want to tell Dick something. Alida is here with me, and she has her baby. Alida. I want you to tell Dick." Silence.

"There is something else she wants to tell us. Something important. Is someone helping her?"

"Yes, there was someone. But she lost the thought, she believed she could get through, and then it all faded. If Walter and Dick could be there to help—"

"Dick is helping."

"Yes, she felt that, just a little, but it is so hard to hold the contact . . . She is gone."

"We are waiting for Louise. Can she come? We hope she'll try to come. She knows there is something important to tell us. Can someone help?"

"Yes—yes—because she was so worried, something to tell the boys the boys the boys because someone was going to hurt Dick. She tried—but it was no use. No use to try."

After ten minutes of silence, DeWitt uttered an annoyed exclamation and turned up the lamp. Cora Delaney had not been in trance; she said, "She seems very confused and lost, poor thing. I have the feeling she's tried so hard to come through, without reaching anyone, she's just given it up. She seems awfully concerned about her boys."

"Yes, she would be," said Jesse. "I've got a little idea." He went out to the anteroom and used the phone.

"Why, sure!" said Bob Walsh, delighted. "You mean I could sit in? Sure, that'd be great, if you think it could help. I'm just sitting here trying to make sense of Latin grammar—if I flunk the course I can always take it over. I'll leave the porch light on for you."

"Just occurred to me," said Jesse in the entry hall where the old clock swung its solemn pendulum, "that she might get through here easier. We don't know anything about the actual mechanism, how the thing works at all. We can guess, from evidence, that on the higher level of vibration they can see through to here, dimly, where we can't see through to them. And this was her house—she might get here easier and feel calmer."

"You've been trying to contact her?" asked Bob. He was excited and interested. "Golly, what Mom is missing. Well, I suppose she might. Of course most of the furniture's different. Where do you want to sit?"

"Let's try the living room," said Jesse.

They put the medium in the largest armchair, switched on a table lamp in the corner of the room, and DeWitt began patiently, "We are waiting for Louise. We want Louise to come and speak to us. She knows what it is we want her to tell us."

After a long silence the medium said quite suddenly, "It wasn't important after she got over, except that it was all wrong here. Something bad for Dick. She wanted to—someone said, rest, but she had to try to get back because of Dick. *Oh!* Where is my Chippendale chair? Where are my lamps? I never had this carpet—" The medium made a strong effort to get out of the chair, and sank back moaning.

"It's all right. Time has passed, this is not your house now," said DeWitt hastily. "Your things are safe, somewhere else."

"Oh. She thought— Wait. She knows that you are here, but what she tried to tell before—before—no one would listen, she went from one person to another to tell them, he didn't, he didn't, wouldn't hurt, and then it was explained to her that no one here could see or hear her, and she felt as though she were going insane— And even when someone helped her to come through—no use, no use, they couldn't understand what she tried to say. She must, must make someone understand—you won't understand. I said it, I know I said it and someone heard me there—I'm sure of it—yes, I understand, concentrate very hard and keep the mind steady—I will—*Those wicked, wicked boys! Those horrible little boys! Oh!*" The medium began to moan again and jerk about in the chair. "I can't I can't I can't—" She gave a little sob, slid half off the chair, and was silent.

DeWitt was over there at once. "Let's have some light." He

felt her pulse, got out his blood-pressure apparatus. "All right," he said after a moment. "She doesn't often get that deep."

"Golly," said Bob in a hushed voice. "Do you think that was Mrs. Tredgold?" He drew a deep breath and looked at Jesse.

Jesse was sitting bolt upright on the couch, his eyes fixed on space. "Mr. Falkenstein?" asked Bob nervously.

"*All iniquity is as a two-edged sword*— My God in heaven," said Jesse. "My God." Slowly he looked around, from Bob's anxious gaze on him, and drew a breath. "Tell me something."

"Sure. What?"

"What," asked Jesse, "became of those boys—the other ones fooling around the block that day? Dave Warren—I forget—"

"I don't know," said Bob. "The Palfreys and Warrens moved —Larry Foster was ahead of me in school, I guess he graduated from Fairfax. That's all I— *Mr. Falkenstein, you don't think—*"

The Fosters still lived around the corner on Larrabee Street. Larry Foster was in his senior year at the University of California at Berkeley.

Records at the junior high school eventually turned up an address for the Warrens. They had moved to Pasadena. Jesse found the place, a more modest house than the one they had left six years before, in the middle of a clear cold afternoon; unusually the back mountains of the Sierra Madre range were visible, and the snow glistened up there like the frosting on a birthday cake. Nobody answered his repeated rings at the door, but as he turned down the front steps a woman was just getting out of a car in the next driveway. She called over to him pleasantly, "Mrs. Warren should be home soon, I think she's just gone to the market."

"I'm really looking for her son Dave. Does he live at home?"

Her mouth dropped in small shock. "Oh—you don't know," she said. "I'm sorry—he's dead. He got on drugs in high school, they tried all sorts of rehabilitation, but it wasn't any use. He died from an overdose of heroin two years ago."

The school records had also provided him with Mrs. Rachel Palfrey's address. Somebody had said, a divorce, a lot of trouble. And that she had worked. By the address, an upper unit in a garish new garden apartment on Fountain Avenue, she probably still worked; he went to see her at seven-thirty that evening.

She opened the door halfway and looked at him. She had undressed, put on a housecoat, but the day's make-up was still in place, smudged, and she looked tired and drawn. She wouldn't be over forty-five or so, but she looked like a woman life had used hard.

"Mrs. Palfrey?"

"Yes, what is it? You'll have to excuse me, I'm not interested—"

"Not selling anything. I'm looking for your son Mike."

She stared at him dully. "Mike?"

"That's right. Do you know where he is?" asked Jesse sharply.

After a minute she said, "Why, yes. I know where Mike is. He's in the death house at Utah State Prison. They're going to execute him next week."

It was nothing like the outside or the inside of the Men's Colony at San Luis Obispo. It was a drab gray forbidding-looking building, and the warden had left Jesse to wait in a small square room with one door and bars on the window; the room smelled of disinfectant.

It had taken two expensive long-distance phone calls and an extremely long explanatory telegram to get him in here, the warden finally accepting his earnest representation that a grave miscarriage of justice could result if he wasn't allowed to see Mike Palfrey. He had flown in from Los Angeles yesterday. There was a lot of snow on the ground in Utah, and it was bitterly cold.

Mike Palfrey, the guard had informed him chattily on the long way across the yard and past several other buildings, richly deserved his waiting fate in front of a firing squad. He had been handed the death penalty for the abduction, robbery, and murder of a middle-aged couple, and murder and rape of their daughter; but he was strongly suspected of having been responsible for at least three other rapes and two murders in California, over a period of several years.

"In this state anyway," said the guard, "we don't fool around with that kind. You can't cure 'em, why keep 'em around?"

Jesse waited for some time before another guard came in and looked him over; he had already been searched for weapons. Satisfied, the guard stepped back and ushered in his prisoner, and sat down himself by the door with eyes alert.

Mike Palfrey, just turned twenty-two, was a stocky, rather good-looking fellow with wiry curling blond hair, quick nervous blue eyes, and a consciously charming smile. He showed that to Jesse and said, "Do I know you, friend? I don't think so. But thanks for relieving the monotony."

"I've got a few questions I hope you'll answer," said Jesse. "If you can remember all the answers."

Mike cocked his head. "Such as?"

"The murder of Mrs. Louise Tredgold. Eight years ago in West Hollywood."

Mike stared at him, and then suddenly threw his head back and began to laugh. "Oh, by God, but I knew it! I knew something would happen to get me out of this hell hole! Oh, by God, that's funny—that's the funniest damned thing ever happened to me! All this time later, somebody finds out about that, so there's got to be all the legal fuss and bother, you got to tie up all the red tape, and they can't put me in front of a firing squad till it's all done! I've always been lucky—let me get back to California, who knows what next?"

"You were lucky that time, anyway," said Jesse. "Just like that, you admit you did that killing?"

"She was the first one," said Mike. "And my God, I never meant to, but that's the way things happen. You got a cigarette?" Jesse gave him one. "So you want to hear about it, I don't mind telling you. You know anything about how it happened?"

"Most of it. You could take it from when you and Dave Warren and Larry Foster came back from the swimming pool that day."

Mike drew strongly on the cigarette. "God, it seems a couple of hundred years back. That day. It was so damned hot. Yeah, we came back to my place, we passed the Tredgold house on the corner, and she wasn't home—I thought she wasn't home, the garage was empty. There was a car in front, but that was Mr. Shellabarger's Buick. We dumped our bathing suits, and I said let's see if we can get into old lady Tredgold's place, just something to do. I'd never pulled a B. and E., thought it might be a fun thing. Dave and Larry weren't so eager, but they came along.

"And, man, it was like we were expected. Back door locked, but the screen was loose on the window in the service porch, I just had to shove it up and raise the window and in we went. Listen, the crazy thing was, we didn't intend to *do* anything— we were punk kids, how'd we know what to do with any loot? We just went in, we were just looking around, and there we were in the living room when she sounded off. I guess she'd heard us from upstairs, anyway there she was—it was funny really—all dressed up she was, and saying, you wicked little boys, what are you doing here?"

Mike laughed again. "Just punk kids," he said. "Dave and Larry were scared as hell, they tried to run, but damn, I knew how Pop 'd belt me again, he find out about that on top of the trouble about that damn fool girl at school—man, she'd been asking for it—I just knew I had to stop the old lady from telling, and while she was making a grab for Dave and Larry I got hold of that poker. Nothing to it, one smack and down she went, but I gave her a couple more to make sure. And then I saw that pin she dropped—I guess she'd just been putting it on—"

"We got out the window again, and man, those two were scared, what'd I do that for, what we do now? I said, for God's sake, what's to do? Nobody could know it was us in there. And nobody ever did. They got some relative of hers for it, it was no sweat." He looked at Jesse, curious now. "How the hell did anybody ever find out?"

"You might be surprised," said Jesse. "And would you mind telling me, Mr. Palfrey, just how I'm going to be sure you're not making up a pretty story to delay your date with the firing squad?"

Mike gave him an amused smile. "So I'll call the bluff," he said. "I told you I was a punk kid then—I didn't know what to do with that diamond pin, didn't know a fence. I was scared Pop would find it. I hid it at the back of the closet in my room —there was a place the baseboard was loose. And when the big split came and Mom walked out and took me with her, I never had a chance to get it. I don't know who bought the house or who's living there now, but the chances are the damned thing might be still there."

The people who had bought the house after the divorce settlement were still there. Their name was Wedemeyer.

The two sheriff's deputies accompanying Jesse formally served the search warrant, and watched indignantly by the Wedemeyers en masse moved a small chest of drawers from the back wall of the closet. The ten-year-old Wedemeyer daughter had the back bedroom. "If you go damaging any paint—" said Wedemeyer. "You just be careful, is all."

They damaged more than that, because she had nailed the loose baseboard neatly in place. One of the deputies pried it up, and as the board pulled away from the furring something dropped and rolled. It didn't sparkle much, because the diamonds were dirty and dull after eight years.

It had been late afternoon when the search warrant had come through, the day after Jesse got back from Utah; it was seven-thirty then, and they went right down to the Tredgolds' in Santa Monica to show them the brooch.

"But that's it!" said Becky. "Of course I'd know it anywhere—where on earth—" The sheriff's deputy told her she'd have to sign a statement about it, and gave her a receipt for it, and they took it away with them. Jesse stayed to tell them about Mike Palfrey.

They listened numbly, unbelieving at first. "I don't know what to say," said Walt Tredgold. "I don't know. Just—leaping to conclusions like that, and it worked out. Who would ever have suspected—"

Jesse eyed him sadly and decided it was an inauspicious time to try to convince him that he had just acted on evidence received.

"What—happens now? If he's confessed, as you say, will they extradite him, or—"

"That's what he thinks," said Jesse. "No, they won't. They were all juveniles, it would have been called second- or third-degree homicide at the time, and we've got a very limited death penalty in this state. We've got Mike Palfrey's deposition, a clear confession to the murder. Dave Warren and Larry Foster would have been charged as accessories—Dave's beyond reach, and it'll be a little shock for Larry, ancient history rising up at him, but nothing 'll happen to him. Contrary to what Mike expects, I doubt very much that this will delay his date with the firing squad by much."

"But Dick—"

"Oh, the governor will issue a pardon," said Jesse, "if that won't offend his principles all over again."

"I still can't take it in—" Suddenly Walt seized Jesse's hand and wrung it fervently. "How we can ever thank you," he muttered, "I don't know. I just don't know. I never expected you could— Like a miracle. I think I ought to tell you—that insurance. We still use the same company, and I know the agent pretty well. I put it in confidence to him, and I've paid it all back—what Uncle Walt got out of that fire." He let out a long sigh.

"How can we ever thank you?" asked Becky emotionally. "It's more than a miracle—"

Jesse, thinking about Nell's new house and all her expanding ideas about redecorating, said absently that money would be fine. Then he grinned at them. "Well, I don't quite believe how it came out either—but I'm glad it worked out the way it did."

"You'll be hearing from Dick—you'll send me a bill." Tredgold wrung his hand again silently.

———————

Nell was going round and round these days with painters and carpenters, looking at carpet samples and upholstery fabrics. When she got home that next afternoon Jesse was on the phone to DeWitt, with Athelstane sitting on his feet listening interestedly to the noises inside the black box.

"Yes, I thought—just a minute." Jesse held the phone away and looked enquiringly at Nell, who had just carried the sleepy baby into the nursery and come back to stand beside him.

"I just wondered if you needed another bottle of Bourbon. Fran and Andrew were coming over after dinner, Andrew wants to hear all about your murder. You know he's been putting in such overtime on this arson thing—"

"There's half a fifth left," said Jesse. "Neither of us can guzzle that in one evening." Nell laughed and went out to start dinner. "You were saying, William?"

"Well, a rather unusual little case," said DeWitt. "I'm writing up an account for our files, of course. You know, I'm tempted to try the manuscript on the Eidlinger Foundation's bi-yearly *Psi Report*. After all—"

"Don't waste the postage," said Jesse. "They're not interested in individual survival any more, William—very old-fashioned, hopelessly nineteenth century. What they're hot on now is statistical runs of the Zenor cards, and kittens in mazes possibly using ESP to find the food dishes."

"Er—you could be right," said DeWitt cautiously. "I'll think it over. But it was quite an interesting case. Quite fairly evidential."

"Mmh yes. 'More things in heaven and earth, Horatio, than are dreamt of—'"

"Really, Jesse," said DeWitt in a pained tone, "can't you think of a less hackneyed quotation?"